Scream Queens
THE MUSICAL

Book, Music and Lyrics
by Scott Martin

A SAMUEL FRENCH ACTING EDITION

SAMUEL FRENCH
FOUNDED 1830

NEW YORK HOLLYWOOD LONDON TORONTO

SAMUELFRENCH.COM

**IMPORTANT BILLING AND CREDIT
REQUIREMENTS**

All producers of *SCREAM QUEENS, THE MUSICAL must* give credit to the Author of the Play in all programs distributed in connection with performances of the Play, and in all instances in which the title of the Play appears for the purposes of advertising, publicizing or otherwise exploiting the Play and/or a production. The name of the Author *must* appear on a separate line on which no other name appears, immediately following the title and *must* appear in size of type not less than fifty percent of the size of the title type.

In addition the following credit *must* be given in all programs and publicity information distributed in association with this piece:

SCREAM QUEENS, THE MUSICAL was developed
with the generous support and cooperation of
The Academy for New Musical Theatre,
The Disney/ASCAP Musical Theatre Workshop,
and The Stages Festival of New Musicals at
Theatre Building Chicago.

SCREAM QUEENS, THE MUSICAL premiered at the Whitefire Theatre in Sherman Oaks, California on October 15th, 1998 for 24 performances.

Cast:

ALEXIS . . . . Lateefah DeVoe

RICHELLE. . . . . Jaime Flowers

NADINE. . . . . Diane Hurley

DEEDEE. . . . . Lisa Ingro

TONYA . . . . JJ Rodgers

BIANCA . . . . Amy Tolsky

Understudies:

RICHELLE/TONYA. . . . . Andrea Adams

DEEDEE/BIANCA . . . . .Susie Singer Carter

ALEXIS/NADINE. . . . . Beverly Sand

SWING. . . . . Adrea Gibbs

Directed by Scott Martin and Adrea Gibbs
Produced by Jayne Hamil
Musical Arrangements by Christopher J. Freyer

ACKNOWLEDGEMENTS

SCREAM QUEENS, THE MUSICAL
was developed with the generous support and cooperation of
John Sparks and the Academy for New Musical Theatre
Stephen Schwartz, Michael Kerker and the Disney/ASCAP Musical
Theatre Workshop
The Stages Festival of New Musicals at Theatre Building Chicago

CHARACTERS

RICHELLE – The cute one; mid-30s; alto; perky, a girl-next-door smile with a girl-on-the-corner body. She was the most popular "Scream Queen" of the late 20th century and is very anxious to revive her career. She has appeared at many dozens of these conventions and originated the idea for tonight's show

NADINE – The British one; mid-50s; alto; sensual yet aloof. She's the senior "Scream Queen" who has seen and done it all, having played everything from a corpse to a vampire princess to a prehistoric tribal maiden to a Playboy centerfold – almost. She's a semi-recovered alcoholic and sneaks a quick drink from a small flask whenever she thinks no one is looking.

BIANCA – The loveable one; late 30s; mezzo; very buxom, good-natured with practical mid-western earthiness. She's happily married with children but never lets the spotlight intrude on her private life. Her occasional clumsiness is due to the size of her breasts and her refusal to wear her eyeglasses in public.

TONYA – The sincere one; late 20s; mezzo; sweet, charismatic, still somewhat naïve. A former Tri-State cheerleading champion, she is the most serious actress of the group and really believes that her B-movie career will lay a foundation for respectable stardom.

DEEDEE – The trashy one; mid-30s; mezzo; intense, edgy, tough on the outside but lonely and desperate within. She wears extreme make-up, hair and clothes to hide her natural beauty, and will do anything to, for and with anybody (including a popular porno video series) to get ahead and be noticed like her idol Traci Lords.

ALEXIS – The smart one; early 40s; alto; compassionate, sisterly, level-headed. She has a college degree, invests carefully and acts as the politician, often refereeing amongst the other Queens. She also has the good business sense to produce her own videos.

"They sing – they dance – they die!"

MUSICAL NUMBERS

SCREAM QUEENS .... All
I GOT ALL OF THE TALENT I NEED .... Richelle, Alexis,
                                                Nadine, DeeDee
FAY WRAY.....................................Tonya (& Others)
GOTCHA CORNERED ....Bianca, DeeDee,
                                                Richelle
STILL IN DEMAND ....Nadine (& Others)
EVERYBODY STARTS AT THE BOTTOM ....Alexis, Bianca,
                                                DeeDee
I'M ALRIGHT, MOMMA.....................Bianca, Nadine, Tonya
SOUTH OF THE BORDER ....Alexis (& Others)
HAPPY ENDINGS .... Richelle
DON'T OPEN THAT DOOR .... DeeDee (& Others)
ROGER CORMAN............................ Bianca (& Others)
SPECIAL FX.. All
REMEMBER THE NAME .... All
FINALE.. All

SCOTT MARTIN has worked extensively for many years in the Los Angeles area as an actor, director, writer and musician. Among his many other successfully-produced musicals are: *Children Of The Night* (the true story of author Bram Stoker's lifelong devotion to the great actor Sir Henry Irving), *Little Green Men* (a youth camp panics on the night of Orson Welles' 'War of the Worlds' radio broadcast), *Bleacher Babes* (the widows of a men's softball team reunite for one last picnic), as well as such family-friendly parodies as *Rockin' Robin Hood, The Road To Paradise, The Maltese Chicken* and *Darn Dodgers*. He has written material for numerous revues and industrial shows, film projects and children's theatre productions, and is a long-time member of ASCAP. For more information visit www.scottmartinmusicals.com

ACT ONE

(**TIME:** *January, 1998*)

(**PLACE:** *The Banquet Room at the Holiday Place Hotel and Convention Center, Parma Heights, Ohio*)

(This is the site of the annual "GlamaGore ScreamiCon," a weekend convention for vendors, collectors, celebrities, and obsessed fans of the direct-to-video horror film genre. The plush walls of the elegant room are covered with the sleazy merchandise of the biz: lurid movie posters and publicity items from such gut-wrenching films as "Invasion of the Bug Eyed Zombies," "Malibu Vampire Vixens," "South Central Chainsaw Sluts," etc.)

(At one side or upstage is a large video screen and speaker system facing the audience. A prop CD boom box is here also.)

*(**NOTE:** the boom box is used to reinforce the cheap production values that the Queens must use for their traveling show and to satisfy the audience's curiosity about "where is the music coming from?" Use at your own discretion only with the pre-recorded music tracks.)*

(If pre-recorded music tracks are used, naturally they should be controlled from the tech booth and amplified through the theatre sound system.)

(If live musicians are used, position them in view of the audience and improvise a few lines of dialogue somewhere in the show to introduce them as characters in the performance; e.g. "This is Tonya's current boyfriend and his garage band who travel with us to all the conventions.")

(At center is a long table with a floor-length skirting, dressed with name cards, water bottles and glossy photos of the Scream Queens.)

(Downstage of the table is an easel with a hand-made sign that reads "Next Show" and a clock face that indicates "8:00" [or starting time of the performance.] Stanchions and velvet ropes separate the audience from the performing area and a large banner hung above reads: "Welcome To The 1998 GlamaGore ScreamiCon." As the audience is being seated, music tracks from various famous horror films [e.g. "Psycho," "The Exorcist," "Halloween"] or original music tracks are played over the theatre sound system.)

(On the stage manager's cue, the booming voice of a smarmy, Las Vegas-type announcer is heard.)

ANNOUNCER. *(off)* LLLLLadies and gentlemen! Welcome to the best – the biggest – the bloodiest, two-day, flesh-ripping, bra-busting festival of hardcore gore and eviscerated excess! Hold onto your hats – and your wallets! It's the International GlamaGore ScreamiCon!!

(The **SCREAM QUEENS** *enter through the back of the theatre, ad-libbing with the crowd, posing for snapshots, signing autographs and basking in their quirky celebrity status. They are wearing a variety of colorful and erotic costumes that showcase their natural assets.)*

(Loaded down with their carry-all bags, the **SCREAM QUEENS** *congregate around the center table, ad-libbing as they unload and unpack. They remove the "Next Show" sign and put the stanchions off to one side.)*

(As the house lights dim, **RICHELLE** *pushes the "play" button on the CD boom box and the music begins.)*

SONG #1: "SCREAM QUEENS"

ANNOUNCER. *(off)* And here they are – direct from Hollywood, California – those hell-raisin' honeys from the Horrorama Hall of Fame. Are you ready for – the Scream Queens!!

(Lights transform the stage into a glitzy rock concert arena as the **QUEENS** *turn, pose for the crowd and sing.)*

TONYA.
> HOW DOES A YOUNG GIRL FRESH FROM HIGH SCHOOL,
> SUDDENLY ON HER OWN,
> FACING THE WORLD ALONE, DAY TO DAY,
> FIND FORTUNE AND FAME?

RICHELLE & DEEDEE.
> MAYBE THE YOUNG GIRL MEETS A GUY
> WHO SAYS SHE CAN BE A STAR.

NADINE & ALEXIS.
> YOU DON'T NEED YEARS OF ACTING CLASS
> TO GET YOU TO EMOTE

BIANCA.
> IF YOU CAN PUSH THAT SOUND
> OUT OF YOUR THROAT.

ALL.
> THAT'S HOW WE GOT TO BE THE
> SCREAM QUEENS!

> *(scream)*

> B-MOVIE BABES JUST MAKIN' A LIVING.
> SCREAM QUEENS!

> *(scream)*

> SHAKIN' OUR TITS AND PAYIN' THE RENT.

RICHELLE.
> EVERYONE USES US.
> NO ONE CONFUSES US WITH SNOW WHITE.

ALL.
> BECAUSE WE'RE
> SCREAM QUEENS, DOIN' A CONVENTION.
> SCREAM QUEENS, DO WE HAVE TO MENTION
> AIN'T NOTHIN' BUT SCREAM QUEENS HERE –
> TONIGHT.

> *(dance break)*

ALEXIS.	**OTHERS.**
I NEVER DREAMED	OOOOO –
THAT ONE DAY I'D BE	RIGHT THERE UP ON
UP ON A MOVIE SCREEN	THE SCREEN.
THERE WHERE I COULD	BY ALL OF MY
BE SEEN IN THE NUDE	FRIENDS.
BY ALL OF MY FRIENDS.	

DEEDEE.

FLEEING FROM PSYCHOS, CAKED IN BLOOD,

ALL.

IT'S HELL, BUT IT'S STILL A JOB.

NADINE.

TO STAY EMPLOYED, WE USE OUR BRAINS.

RICHELLE & BIANCA.

YES, WE DO.

DEEDEE.

SOME OF US USE OUR TONGUES.

TONYA. *(indicating* **DEEDEE,** *spoken:)* She does!

RICHELLE.

BUT IF YOU'VE GOT

A HEALTHY PAIR OF LUNGS –

NADINE.

YOU NEED A HEALTHY PAIR OF LUNGS –

ALEXIS.

YOU NEED A HEALTHY PAIR OF LUNGS –

DEEDEE.

YOU NEED A HEALTHY PAIR OF LUNGS –

TONYA.

YOU NEED A HEALTHY PAIR OF LUNGS –

BIANCA.

I'VE GOT A HEALTHY PAIR –

(For a beat, the **OTHERS** *eye her large breasts.)*

ALL.

– OF LUNGS!

THAT'S ALL IT TAKES TO BE A
SCREAM QUEEN!

(scream)

B-MOVIE BABES JUST MAKIN' A LIVING.
SCREAM QUEENS!

(scream)

SHAKIN' OUR TITS AND PAYIN' THE RENT.
STARE AT THIS HEAVING BUST,

ENVIOUS OR WITH LUST, THAT'S ALRIGHT.
BECAUSE WE'RE
SCREAM QUEENS, HERE ON EXHIBITION.
SCREAM QUEENS, FREE WITH THE ADMISSION.
YOU'RE GETTIN' TO SEE
YOUR FAV'RITE SCREAM QUEENS HERE –
TONIGHT –.

(After the applause, stage lights return to normal as **RICHELLE** *pushes the "stop" button on the boom box and addresses the audience as the* **OTHERS** *return to the table.)*

RICHELLE. Thank you and welcome to the "elegant" Holiday Place Hotel and Convention Center here in beautiful, snow-covered Parma, Ohio. This is really something. I mean, how many three-star hotels have their own bowling alley?

(The sounds of a bowling alley come from the back of the theatre.)

Could we keep that door closed back there?

(The sound of a door slamming comes from the back of the theatre.)

This is the seventh annual International GlamaGore ScreamiCon.

(counts on her fingers to be sure)

Wow! Seven years ago I'd just done "Return of the Chainsaw Nurses" and last week I finished "Return of the Chainsaw Nurses – Part 7!" Doesn't seem possible!

(The **OTHERS** *cross downstage.)*

TONYA. For those of you way in the back, I'm Tonya; three-time winner of "Fangaworld" magazine's "Screamer of the Year" Award!

*(***RICHELLE*** *prompts the audience to applaud after each intro.)*

ALEXIS. Alexis; writer-producer and star of that hot direct-to-video series, "Witch Bitch."

NADINE. Nadine; those unfamiliar with my long list of credits, you are definitely at the wrong convention!

DEEDEE. DeeDee; some of you might not recognize me with this many clothes on.

BIANCA. And Bianca; watch for my latest video called "Bikini Babes from Beyond" – comin' at ya in 3-D!

(wiggles her breasts)

RICHELLE. And for anyone not into chainsaws, I'm Richelle!

BIANCA. *(teasing)* Not THE Richelle?! The most popular B-movie horror star of all time?!

NADINE. *(teasing)* Where have you been, dahling? You used to be big!

RICHELLE. *(posing, a la Norma Desmond)* I am big! It's the videos that got small.

(holds up a DVD)

And all of mine are for sale in the lobby!

OTHERS. And ours!

DEEDEE. Even my hardcore titles, but we have to see some I.D.

TONYA. Tonight is a special moment for us. We've done lots of videos with each other but this is the first time the six of us have appeared together live.

RICHELLE. Live! That's the keyword here. My manager says to me, "All-girl groups are the hottest thing right now. So why don't you get your friends together and go out on tour? Can they sing?"

*(The **OTHERS** pose.)*

"Can they dance?"

*(The **OTHERS** pose again.)*

"Can they fake it?"

OTHERS. Heyyy –

NADINE. So here we are trying out our "specialty material."

BIANCA. We wrote most of it ourselves.

TONYA. A couple guys in my musical theatre class did the songs, but we had to figure out the talking parts.

DEEDEE. Every Hollywood writer we called just hung up on us.

ALEXIS. Except Joan Rivers. We hung up on her!

RICHELLE. So now we get to appear at this super-cool convention.

ALEXIS. But just our luck, they double-booked the room. There's a Polish wedding reception in here at ten so we gotta keep it moving!

(A cell phone rings, and the QUEENS run to their bags and pull out their cell phones.)

ALL. *(perky business voices)* Hello?

TONYA. Mine. 'Scuse me.

(TONYA turns upstage, miming a phone conversation, as the OTHERS put the phones away in their bags.)

RICHELLE. Later on tonight in the Blue Pierogi Room, they're screening a rough cut of that upcoming horror film, "I Saw What You Did And Why Didn't You Clean It Up?" – written and directed by that brilliant new Hollywood boy wonder – Spike Spiegleman!

(The OTHERS, except TONYA, squeal excitedly.)

Now Spike – if you're out there – I read this week in "The Hollywood Reporter" that you're casting for your next project. Why waste time auditioning young no-name babes when you've got the best right here, right now? We've been running and screaming and dying on video for years! All we want is a chance to move up into a classier picture.

ALEXIS. One where WE don't have to move the lighting equipment between set-ups.

RICHELLE. So what do you say, Spike? Give us an audition and we will BLOW you away!

DEEDEE. OR we could just –

RICHELLE, ALEXIS, NADINE, BIANCA. Don't say it.

TONYA. *(closes her phone, annoyed)* That was my manager. I didn't get a single death threat this week!

RICHELLE. You hear that, Spike? This little lady's popularity has sunk so low even her stalker is losing interest! How about a good part in a good movie?

NADINE. I haven't had a really good part in ages; not since my hey-day as queen of the drive-in theater circuit.

BIANCA. That's how I started; teenage beach party movies. They were looking for extras who could fill out a bikini.

NADINE. Fill it?? Dahling, you stuffed the hell out of it.

(**RICHELLE** *pushes the "play" button on the boom box and the music begins.*)

SONG #2: "I GOT ALL OF THE TALENT I NEED"

RICHELLE. And that's something the fans are always curious about. How DID we get started in the movies?

ALEXIS. It just came natural to me.

DEEDEE. Me, too.

(**BIANCA** *and* **TONYA** *exit as* **NADINE, ALEXIS, DEEDEE** *and* **RICHELLE** *line up like Follies girls.*)

ALL.

SOME OF US GIRLS ARE MEANT TO BE
SADDLED WITH HOME AND FAMILY.

RICHELLE.

SOME OF US WASH THE SHEETS.

DEEDEE.

SOME OF US WORK THE STREETS.

ALEXIS.

SOME OF US REACH FOR GREAT CAREERS

NADINE.

WHILE SOME OF US ROAM THE AISLES AT SEARS.

RICHELLE & DEEDEE.

BUT SOONER OR LATER WE LEAVE THE NEST

ALEXIS & NADINE.

TO FACE THE CHALLENGE AND TAKE THE TEST.

ALL.

STICK OUT OUR CHIN, THROW OUT OUR CHEST,

(They do.)

AND LEARN WHAT WE DO BEST.

ALEXIS.

I'VE GOT A COLLEGE DEGREE IN MICROBIOLOGY,
BUT AS A DOCTOR, I'D NEVER SUCCEED.
BUT LET ME STAR IN A HORROR MOVIE
AND I GOT ALL OF THE TALENT I NEED.

RICHELLE.

I ALWAYS FAILED TO PASS MY SECRETARIAL CLASS
BECAUSE I NEVER COULD TYPE UP TO SPEED.
BUT LET ME STAR IN A HORROR MOVIE
AND I GOT ALL OF THE TALENT I NEED.

NADINE.

YOU HAVE TO FIND OUT WHAT YOU ARE SUITED
FOR
UPON THIS MERRY-GO-ROUND OF LIFE.
AND WE HAVE FOUND THAT WHAT WE ARE SUITED
FOR
ARE REPEATED ATTACKS WITH AN AX OR A KNIFE.

DEEDEE.

I TRIED TO SELL "MARY KAY," THAT ONLY LASTED A
DAY.
I GOT SO NERVOUS AND SCARED THAT I PEED.
BUT LET ME STAR IN A HORROR MOVIE,

DEEDEE & ALEXIS.

A LOUSY LOW-BUDGET HORROR MOVIE,

DEEDEE, ALEXIS & NADINE.

JUST LET ME STAR IN A HORROR MOVIE,

RICHELLE.

BECAUSE WITH ALL OF MY SKILLS
THEN I'LL PAY ALL OF MY BILLS.

ALL.

YEAH, I GOT ALL OF THE TALENT I NEED.

(Soft-shoe dance break a la Fred Astaire, using plastic long-handled doubled-headed axes as "canes," then **ALEXIS** *poses as the Frankenstein monster.)*

ALEXIS. Arrrrrgh!!

ALL.

> AND I GOT ALL OF THE TALENT I NEED.

(Dance break, then **NADINE** *poses as Dracula.)*

NADINE. "Cheeldrun ov dee night – vhat music dey make!"

ALL.

> AND I GOT ALL OF THE TALENT I NEED.

DEEDEE.

> THEY SAY THAT EVERYONE HAS A SPECIAL GIFT
> THAT IS IMPOSSIBLE TO REPLACE.
> AND WE ARE PROUD TO SAY THAT OUR SPECIAL
> GIFT
> IS SCREAMING ON CUE 'TIL WE'RE BLUE IN THE
> FACE.

ALL. Eeek! Oooo! Eeeek!

> SOMETIMES WE GET TO DO BITS IN MAJOR STUDIO
> HITS
> 'CAUSE NO ONE THINKS WE CAN HANDLE THE LEAD.
> BUT WHEN WE STAR IN A HORROR MOVIE
> THEN WE GOT ALL OF THE TALENT WE NEED.
>
> WE NEVER WORRY A LOT ABOUT THE STORY OR
> PLOT.
> OUR FANS ARE HAPPY AS LONG AS WE BLEED.

DEEDEE.

> THEY WANNA SEE US IN HORROR MOVIES.

NADINE.

> CAN'T GET ENOUGH OF THOSE HORROR MOVIES.

ALEXIS.

> SO WE KEEP MAKIN' MORE HORROR MOVIES.

RICHELLE.

> AND WHILE US B-MOVIE BROADS
> AIN'T WINNIN' ANY AWARDS

ALL.

> WE STILL GOT ALL THE TALENT WE NEED –.

(After the applause, the lights change as **DEEDEE**,
RICHELLE, **NADINE** *and* **ALEXIS** *exit and* **TONYA** *enters
from the opposite side, addressing the crowd.)*

TONYA. I was four years old when Mom entered me in the Pottawatomie County pre-school beauty and talent pageant.

#2-A: Underscore

I had to sing, wear a pink ballerina's costume and call in fifty-two spotted hogs from a field half a mile away.

(The music stops and **TONYA** *does an ear-splitting hog call. After several seconds, she coughs and chokes.)*

I lost!

(Underscore music continues.)

But it was my first taste of applause and I've been tryin' to top that performance ever since. By the time I turned seventeen, I was crowned "Miss Cornbread," "Miss Creamed Corn" and "Miss North County Corndog Queen." It was time to get outta Kansas. A road trip with some friends after high school brought me to the West Coast and I met a couple of film students shooting on Santa Monica beach.

(The music stops.)

They introduced me to the joys of Los Angeles theatre. I was in the first and only topless production of *Our Town.* And then my film career was off and running – so to speak.

*(***TONYA*** *pushes the "stop" button on the boom box as the video screen lights up with a scene from one of her early movies where she is running from a stalker through the woods.)*

TONYA'S DEMO REEL: (see author's notes)

(After the last scene, the video screen goes dark and **TONYA** *moves into a special light.)*

TONYA. Sometimes the script looks better on paper that it does on the screen. Sometimes the script isn't even on paper. We just make it up as we go. More than a little talent, it takes confidence, desire and a whole lot of inspiration.

(pushes the "play" button on the boom box, and the music begins)

SONG #3: "FAY WRAY"

And MY inspiration came from watching the midnight creature feature on the only TV station in Pottawatomie County.

I WANNA BE LIKE FAY WRAY,
THE PERFECT DAMSEL IN DISTRESS.
CLUTCHED IN THE HAND OF A BIG HAIRY APE
WEARING NOT MUCH OF A DRESS.
WHEN SHE GOT INTO TROUBLE,
THEY'D HAVE A HERO SET HER FREE.
I WANNA BE LIKE FAY WRAY
AND HAVE SOMEONE RESCUE ME.

  I WILL NEVER FORGET THE DAY
  I FIRST SAW THE MOVIE "KING KONG."
  FAY IS TIED UP BEHIND THE GATE
  OUT IN FRONT OF THAT GONG.
  FROM THE JUNGLE YOU HEAR THE FOOTSTEPS
  THEN SEE THE MONKEY APPEAR.
  FAY STARTS TO SCREAM HER HEAD OFF,
  WHICH INSPIRED MY WHOLE CAREER.

AND THAT'S WHY
I WANNA BE LIKE FAY WRAY
WITH MANY LOVERS ON THE SCREEN.
DINING WITH LEO AND DANCING WITH BRAD
AND THEN SCREWING CHARLIE SHEEN.
WHAT IF THIS KID FROM KANSAS
COULD SEE HER NAME ON SOME MARQUEE?
I WANNA BE LIKE FAY WRAY
AND HAVE SOMEONE NOTICE ME.

  FAY WAS SLENDER AND FAY WAS POUTY
  AND FAY COULD BE SUCH A TEASE.
  SHE AUDITIONED LIKE LADIES SHOULD;
  NEVER DOWN ON HER KNEES.

  FAY'S THE IDOL OF EVERY SCREAM QUEEN.
  TODAY WE'RE ALL IN HER DEBT.

SO IF I FEEL LIKE QUITTING,
THAT'S WHEN I KNOW I CAN'T FORGET

JUST HOW MUCH
I WANNA BE LIKE FAY WRAY
AND SEE THE WORLD FROM THE TOP.
FAY DID HER JOB LIKE THE PRO THAT SHE WAS
AND THEN KNEW JUST WHEN TO STOP.
SHE FOUND A GUY TO MARRY
AND THEN RETIRED AS HIS WIFE.
I WANNA BE LIKE FAY WRAY
AND DO THE SAME THING WITH MY LIFE.

(The **OTHERS** *enter, dancing with plush toy gorillas in their hands.)*

ALL.

I WANNA BE LIKE FAY WRAY,
THE PERFECT DAMSEL IN DISTRESS.
CLUTCHED IN THE HAND OF A BIG HAIRY APE
WEARING NOT MUCH OF A DRESS.
WHEN SHE GOT INTO TROUBLE
THEY'D HAVE A HERO SET HER FREE.
I WANNA BE LIKE FAY WRAY
AND HAVE EVERYONE REMEMBER ME –.

(After the applause, the lights return to normal, the **OTHERS** *put the gorillas underneath the table and* **ALEXIS** *pushes the "stop" button on the boom box.)*

ALEXIS. Just a reminder: later on in the show, we're presenting a special Lifetime Achievement Award to a very famous Hollywood celebrity; someone whose name is synonymous with low-budget horror films and videos; someone who's inspired generations of fans, actors, directors and writers with his low-budget horror films and videos; someone –

DEEDEE, NADINE, BIANCA, TONYA. – who's never hired any of US to be in his low-budget horror films and videos –

RICHELLE. – unlike his very shy protégé, Spike Spiegelman, who can't wait to put us in his new movie, can you baby? Ohh, where are you hiding?

BIANCA. Speaking of videos, remember that two per cent of your purchase price of any of our videos tonight goes directly to a charitable cause that is near and dear to all of our hearts. It's the "Scream Queens' Help Save Our Little Furry Friends Society."

#3-A: The SQHSOLFFS

(*The* **OTHERS** *join hands upstage of her and hum solemnly.*)

We all sincerely believe in the prevention of the cruelty to animals, which is why the SQHSOLFFS is so important in our daily lives. In these terrible times of trouble and strife, the least we can do is make sure that never, ever in our films will you see a helpless little animal being tortured or abused or stepped on or killed or mistreated in any way.

(*The humming stops.*)

RICHELLE. We just save that stuff for the actors.

BIANCA. Oh, but that's entertainment! Anyway – end of commercial. On with the show!

(**NADINE** *steps downstage carrying a Neiman-Marcus shopping bag, as the* **OTHERS** *exit.*)

NADINE. Let's dig into the old mailbag and see if one of our many fans has written us anything we can read out loud.

(*pulls an envelope from the bag and a bloody ear falls out onto the floor*)

Oh, dear. We'll just mark that one "return to sender."

(*puts ear and envelope into bag and pulls out another envelope*)

Why, here's a fan letter for Alexis!

(*looks nervously offstage*)

For Alexis!

(**ALEXIS** *runs onstage, stops, smiles, and crosses to her.*)

From Saginaw, Michigan; look how cute; all printed in crayon; must be from one of your younger fans.

(reads)

"Dear Alexis: I'm doing three life terms for butchering my uncle."

(reacts for a beat)

"I was careful to use the same power tools that worked so good in your film "Revenge of the Post-Menopausal Nanny." You got the inheritance. I got solitary. Where did I go wrong?"

(delicately hands the letter and envelope to **ALEXIS***, and exits with the mailbag)*

ALEXIS. Well – this sounds like another example of life imitating art – or in the case of our films – life imitating late night cable TV filler. I think there's an important lesson to be learned here by all of us. The violence, the gore, the sexism –

(a la William Shatner on "Saturday Night Live")

– it's only a stupid movie, you people! Get a life.

*(***ALEXIS*** exits as* **BIANCA***,* **DEEDEE***. and* **RICHELLE** *enter from the opposite side wearing tights and colorful leotards.)*

BIANCA. Good advice for everybody! We get a lot of strange letters from our fans. Some, we answer; some, we forward to the FBI. But the other day a fan on the street asked me: "Bianca, you are the mother of twins and you're pushin' forty! How do you stay in such great shape?" Well – after makin' a mental note to remove the birthdate from my website – I looked him straight in the eye and said – like any athlete, we Scream Queens have to condition the special areas of our bodies that we use the most.

(pushes the "play" button on the boom box and the music starts)

SONG #4: "GOTCHA CORNERED"

It depends on whether we're getting killed from the front, getting killed from the back, getting killed from the side; whatever the script calls for. For instance, you are –

> WALKING HOME THE STREETS ARE GETTING DARK.
> YOU CAN SAVE TIME
> CUTTING STRAIGHT THROUGH THE PARK.
> AND YOU HAVE DONE IT BEFORE
> AND YOU NEVER HAD ANY TROUBLE.
> JUST BEYOND THE NEAREST EXIT GATE
> SOMEONE STEPS OUT FROM A '68 CHEVY.
> HE'S BREATHING HEAVY.

(**BIANCA, RICHELLE** *and* **DEEDEE** *move as if in an aerobic exercise video.*)

BIANCA, RICHELLE, DEEDEE.

> LOOK OUT, HE'S GOTCHA CORNERED BY THE
> FOUNTAIN;
> GOTCHA CORNERED BY THE TRASH BIN;
> GOTCHA CORNERED AND YOU'RE ALL ALONE.

RICHELLE & DEEDEE.

> BABY, BABY, WHATCHA DOIN' OUT ALONE?

BIANCA.

> GIVE HIM THIS!
> GIVE HIM THAT!
> TAKE HIM DOWN ON YOUR OWN

RICHELLE & DEEDEE.

> WHEN YOU ARE

BIANCA, RICHELLE & DEEDEE.

> CORNERED ALL ALONE.

BIANCA. It ain't easy fightin' off monsters and aliens and psychos take after take. A girl can get hurt if she's not careful. One scene I remember, the script said –

> MOM AND DAD HAVE LEFT FOR MALIBU.
> YOU HAVE GOT
> A BOOK REPORT THAT IS DUE

AND YOU'RE DETERMINED TO STAY UP
ALL NIGHT 'TIL YOU FINISH READING.
SUDDENLY YOU WONDER WHY THE WHOLE
HOUSE IS SOUNDING LIKE A QUIET MUSEUM.
AND THEN YOU SEE HIM.

BIANCA, RICHELLE & DEEDEE.
LOOK OUT, HE'S GOTCHA CORNERED IN THE
KITCHEN;
GOTCHA CORNERED IN THE BEDROOM;
GOTCHA CORNERED AND YOU'RE ALL ALONE.

RICHELLE & DEEDEE.
BABY, BABY, WHY YOU IN THE HOUSE ALONE?

BIANCA.
MAKE HIM HURT!
MAKE HIM HEAVE!
MAKE HIM GRUMBLE AND GROAN

RICHELLE & DEEDEE.
WHEN YOU ARE

BIANCA, RICHELLE & DEEDEE.
CORNERED ALL ALONE.

(The music underscores in disco rhythm variations as they demonstrate more ridiculous self-defense exercises.)

BIANCA. This is a warm-up for when you're looking around for your killer. He could be anywhere!

(first exercise)

This is good practice for when you're being chased through the woods and you have to push away the tree branches.

(different exercise)

And this tummy trimmer is good for when you're calling the police and you drop the phone!

(different exercise)

This is great for when you're running away from a killer and you get your foot stuck in a hole.

(different exercise)

And this builds up your stamina for when the budget is so low you have to run in front of a blue screen.

(different exercise)

And of course this is essential for when you're swimming away from sharks and piranhas and you want to signal for help at the same time.

(different exercise)

BIANCA, RICHELLE & DEEDEE.
LOOK OUT, HE'S GOTCHA CORNERED IN THE BACK SEAT;
GOTCHA CORNERED IN THE HOT TUB;
GOTCHA CORNERED AND YOU'RE ALL ALONE.
RICHELLE & DEEDEE.
BABY, BABY, NEVER TAKE A CHANCE ALONE.
BIANCA.
GET A CLUB.
GET A GUN.
GET A CELLULAR PHONE
RICHELLE & DEEDEE.
WHEN YOU ARE
BIANCA, RICHELLE & DEEDEE.
CORNERED ALL ALONE –.

*(After the applause, **BIANCA**, **DEEDEE** and **RICHELLE** exit as **TONYA** enters from the opposite side, followed by **NADINE**, who pushes the "stop" button on the boom box.)*

TONYA. When I first moved to Southern California, I never realized they had so much culture. I mean, there are so many museums! The Getty, the Norton Simon –

NADINE. The Wax.

TONYA. So now – to bring a little Scream Queen culture to this convention – we proudly present "The Gallery of Ghouls." Our tribute to the immortal ladies of the silver screen who inspire all of us to – keep on screaming!

#4-A: Gallery of Ghouls #1

*(As **NADINE** pushes the "play" button on the boom box, the lights blackout and we hear a scratchy 78 rpm recording of a "Pomp and Circumstance"-like theme and the sound of the Queens' scuffling feet finding their marks on the stage in the dark. Special lights come up, revealing **TONYA** holding a large poster of "The Bride of Frankenstein." She pulls it away, revealing **ALEXIS** dressed and posed like a wax figure in the same position as Elsa Lanchester. **TONYA** prompts the audience to applaud. The lights fade-out, **TONYA** and **ALEXIS** scuffle off in the dark, and the music ends.)*

*(As the lights return to normal, **NADINE** steps forward and pushes the "stop" button on the boom box.)*

NADINE. *(with a hint of sarcasm)* Well – THAT was inspiring. I'd like to set the record straight about some things the fan magazines have written about me over the years. Yes, I was born in Southampton, England. Yes, I turned down the role of Octopussy. And, no, Wilt Chamberlain and I were always just good friends.

(The stage lights dim as the video screen lights up with highlights of her career.)

NADINE'S DEMO REEL: (see author's notes)

(After the last clip, the screen goes dark and the stage lights return to normal.)

And, yes, it's true. I was selected as "Playboy's" Miss September, 1977 – almost. Hef and I got into the most terrible row about where to put the staple.

(indicates on her body)

Here? Here? Good God, not there! So he chose some other Playmate and it didn't hinder my career one bit. Though at my age, it's amazing I even HAVE a career! I love the work, even if it is hell on my personal life.

(pushes the "play" button on the boom box and the music begins)

SONG #5: "STILL IN DEMAND"

In fact, just a few weeks ago –
　IT WAS CHRISTMAS TIME IN HOLLYWOOD
　AND I GET A CALL FROM MY OL' MUM.
　SHE SAYS, "DAHLING, OH, HOW JOLLY WOULD IT BE
　IF HOME, THIS ONCE, YOU'D COME."
　BUT I JUST STARTED DOING A MOVIE
　THAT WILL SHOOT THROUGH THE FIRST OF THE
　YEAR.
　SO, MOTHER, PLEASE MAKE AMENDS
　TO MY FAMILY AND FRIENDS,
　BUT I MUST SPEND CHRISTMAS HERE.

BECAUSE I'M STILL IN DEMAND.
YES, I'M STILL IN DEMAND.
FIFTY AND HOLDING, NO TUCKING OR FOLDING
AND PERFECTLY TANNED.
ACTING IN THE MOVIES FOR A LIVING IS A QUIRK.
WAITRESS OR A CLERK?
NOT ME; I WORK!

STILL IN DEMAND.
YES, I'M STILL IN DEMAND.
AGING, BUT KNOWING IT ISN'T YET SHOWING,
AND ISN'T IT GRAND?
SCREAM QUEENS OVER FORTY USUALLY FIND SOME
NEW CAREER.
BUT I'M STILL IN DEMAND THIS YEAR.

I had monsters chasing me before some of you were
even born!
　ONE OF THE EARLIEST FILMS I APPEARED IN,
　I GOT TO BE DRACULA'S BRIDE.
　CHRISTOPHER LEE TOOK A BITE OUTTA ME
　AND BY PAGE TWENTY-THREE, I DIED.

　I WORKED FOR THE HOTTEST ITALIAN DIRECTORS
　AND NONE COULD REMEMBER MY NAME,
　'TIL MARIO BAVA SAID, "BABY YOU HAVE-A
　BAZOOMS THAT COULD BRING-A YOU FAME!"

AND I'M STILL DEMAND.
YES, I'M STILL IN DEMAND.
BOYS WHO WERE RAUNCHY, NOW BALDING AND
PAUNCHY,
STILL GIVE ME A HAND.
EACH FILM THAT I STARRED IN HAD AT LEAST ONE
SHOWER SCENE.
NOTHING TOO OBSCENE;
"PG" –

(beat, then reluctantly)

Thirteen!

STILL IN DEMAND.
NOW I'M STILL IN DEMAND
BY TWELVE-YEAR-OLD GAWKERS WHO THINK I HAVE
KNOCKERS
FROM FANTASYLAND,
THANKS TO THE SUPPORT FROM ALL MY FANS – AND
MY BRASSIERE,
I AM STILL IN DEMAND THIS YEAR.

In the 80s, an aging Scream Queen had to take any
part she could get.

HORROR WAS DEAD IN THE WATER
UNTIL JANET'S DAUGHTER DID "HALLOWEEN."
SLASHERS AND PSYCHOS AND SICKOS WERE
SUDDENLY
EVERYWHERE ON THE SCREEN.
THAT WAS THE FAD THAT REVIVED MY CAREER.
I DID DOZENS OF CAMEO BITS.
TO GET SPECIAL BILLING, BEFORE EVERY KILLING,
I WILLINGLY WIGGLED MY –

(after a beat, with dignity)

TITS!

(The **OTHERS** *enter with cheap props and costume
pieces, fluttering around her in a mock-glamorous Busby
Berkeley-like finale.)*

OTHERS.	NADINE.

SHE IS STILL IN DEMAND.
YES, SHE'S STILL IN DEMAND.
FIFTY AND HOLDING, NO
TUCKING OR FOLDING,
AND PERFECTLY TANNED.
ACTING IN THE MOVIES FOR   AH-HAA – AH-HAA
A LIVING IS A QUIRK.   – AH-HAA –
WAITRESS OR A CLERK?

                            NOT ME! I WORK!

OTHERS.

SHE'S STILL IN DEMAND.
YES, SHE'S STILL IN DEMAND.
AGING, BUT KNOWING IT ISN'T YET SHOWING,
AND ISN'T IT GRAND?

NADINE.

THREE CHEERS FOR THE LADY WHOM I SEE THERE
IN THE MIRROR.

ALL.

FOR SHE'S / I'M STILL IN THE GREATEST DEMAND –
THIS YEAR –.

(After the applause, a cell phone rings again. The **QUEENS** *throw down their props, run to the table and pull the cell phones from their bags.)*

ALL. *(perky business voices)* Hello?

DEEDEE. Mine.

*(***DEEDEE*** *turns away for her conversation as* **RICHELLE** *pushes the "stop" button on the boom box and the* **OTHERS** *put the phones back in their bags and put the props under the table.)*

RICHELLE. Just for the record, Tonya did all the choreography for that number.

BIANCA. And I sewed the costumes.

RICHELLE. You wouldn't believe how much hidden talent is up here.

ALEXIS. You hear that, Spike? Hidden talent. Up here.

NADINE. Ready, willing and able.

RICHELLE. All kinds of talent.

(They turn and listen to **DEEDEE**'s *conversation.)*

DEEDEE. *(into phone)* Oh, yeah, baby – do it for me. That's it. Don't stop. You can do it. I wanna hear you. Oh, yes, yes, yes, yes! Such a good boy. Gotta go now.

(puts phone away as **OTHERS** *stare at her)*

Hey! It's five ninety-five a minute! I'm on call, twenty-four seven.

RICHELLE. Where was I?

BIANCA & NADINE. All kinds of talent.

RICHELLE. And plenty of it. It ain't easy letting out a blood-curdling scream on cue. And to prove my point, we've got some amateur screamers here in the audience tonight who think they've got the right stuff.

(pushes the "play" button on the boom box and the music begins)

#5-A: SQ Theme

*(**NOTE:** either the* **QUEENS** *ask for volunteers and select three people from the audience to come onstage, or contestants are chosen from a sign-up sheet posted in the lobby before the show.)*

(When the contestants are onstage, **NADINE**, **BIANCA**, **ALEXIS** *and* **DEEDEE** *exit as* **RICHELLE** *pushes the "stop" button on the boom box. The music stops.)*

*(**TONYA** and* **RICHELLE** *quickly ad-lib, "Who are you, where are you from," "What makes you scream," etc. with the three contestants.)*

RICHELLE. *(cont.)* Now, we don't want to discourage you, but I think you should hear what a real butt-clenching Scream Queen scream sounds like. And who better to demonstrate than that three-time "Fangaworld" Award winner herself – Tonya!

*(**RICHELLE** coaxes the audience to applaud for* **TONYA**, *then prompts them to count "1-2-3."* **TONYA**. *lets loose*

with a real ear-popper and bows to the applause.
RICHELLE *and* **TONYA** *tease and ad-lib with each contestant and get them to "scream" one at a time. They select a "winner" with audience applause and give the winner a packet of "Scream Queens' Throat Lozenges."*
RICHELLE *pushes the "play" button on the boom box, playing the SQ Theme again as the contestants return to their seats and* **TONYA** *exits.* **RICHELLE** *pushes the "stop" button on the boom box and the music ends.)*

RICHELLE. *(cont.)* You never know where the next mega-star is gonna come from. Hollywood is built on the hidden talents of people like *(winner's name)*; people who always had it but never got to show it until they were picked out of a crowd. That's why I never, ever forget the advice I got as a little girl when I snuck backstage at our hometown concert hall to see my idol – Miss Diana Ross!

(pushes the "play" button on the boom box and the music begins)

SONG #6: "EVERYBODY STARTS AT THE BOTTOM"

(The stage lights change to look like a 60s rock concert. **RICHELLE** *exits as* **ALEXIS, DEEDEE** *and* **BIANCA** *enter dressed as The Supremes.)*

ALEXIS.
EVERYBODY STARTS AT THE BOTTOM.
NOBODY IS BORN A STAR.
EVERY DAY YOU GOTTA FIND A WAY
TO SHOW THEM WHO YOU ARE.

ALEXIS, DEEDEE & BIANCA.
EVERYBODY STARTS AT THE BOTTOM
BEFORE THEY MAKE IT TO THE TOP.
IF YOU'RE SMART, SAY "YES" TO ANY PART,
EVEN IF THE FILM IS A FLOP.

ALEXIS.
MANY STARS BEGAN IN HORROR FILMS
WHEN THEY WERE HUNGRY FOR A JOB.
CLINT EASTWOOD TARGETED TARANTULAS

AND STEVE MCQUEEN FOUGHT OFF A BLOB.
JACK NICHOLSON TOOK OFF WITH HIS CAREER
WHEN HE DID "LITTLE SHOP OF HORRORS."
WHEN I LOOK AT HIS, AND I LOOK AT OURS,
I REMEMBER MAMA SAID,

ALEXIS.

YES, SUCCESS IS JUST A
STEADY CLIMB.
SHE SAID, WHEN YOU'RE
YOUNG
AND ON THE LOWEST RUNG,
TAKE ONE STEP AT A TIME.

MAMA SAID –

THAT'S HOW YOU GOTTA
PLAY THE GAME.
AND NEVER SQUAWK ABOUT
THE KIND OF SCHLOCK
YOU MUST DO BEFORE
YOU'RE A NAME.

DEMI MOORE GOT PAID A
WHOLE LOT LESS
WHEN SHE APPEARED IN
"PARASITE."
POOR JAMIE LEE SURVIVED
THE "TERROR TRAIN"
BUT HAD A CHEAP DATE ON
"PROM NIGHT."
AND GEENA DAVIS
COULDN'T
HELP BUT CRY
WHENEVER JEFF BECAME
A "FLY."
IF THEY STILL GET WORK,
BABY, SO CAN I.
AND REMEMBER MAMA SAID,
EVERYBODY STARTS AT
THE BOTTOM.

DEEDEE & BIANCA.
EVERYBODY STARTS AT
THE BOTTOM.
SUCCESS IS JUST A
STEADY CLIMB.
WHEN!

JUST TAKE IT ONE –
ONE AT A TIME, YES!
EVERYBODY STARTS AT
THE BOTTOM.
THAT'S HOW YOU GOTTA
PLAY THE GAME.
WAH, WAH,
WAH-OO, WAH-OO,
YOU MUST DO BEFORE
YOU'RE A NAME.

OOOO,
WAH, WAH, WAH *(etc.)*

AHHH –

EVERYBODY STARTS AT
THE BOTTOM.

AND AFTER YOU HAVE PAID

YOUR DUES,
SHE SAID, LIFE'S A BALL
UNLESS YOU BLOW IT ALL
ON CLOTHES AND DRUGS
AND BOOZE.
MAMA SAID –

GOTTA GIVE BEFORE
YOU TAKE.
AND DON'T LOSE SIGHT OF
WHAT YOU DREAM
TONIGHT.
TOMORROW YOU JUST
MIGHT
GET A BREAK.

SISSY SPACEK AND AMY
IRVING
AND JOHN TRAVOLTA
STARRED
IN "CARRIE."
JULIA LOUIS-DREYFUS WAS A
NAKED NYMPH IN "TROLL."
BROOKE SHIELDS WAS
"ALICE,
SWEET, ALICE,"
YOUNG AND SCARY.
SO MANY NO ONES BECAME
SOMEONES
AFTER A HORROR MOVIE
ROLE.

OHH, BABY, BABY;
WHERE DID MY AGENT GO?

OH, YOU CAN'T HURRY
FAME.
YOU JUST HAVE TO WAIT.

SHE SAID

AND AFTER YOU HAVE
PAID
YOUR DUES,
LIFE!
YOU BLOW IT ALL –

LISTEN TO MAMA.
EVERYBODY STARTS AT
THE BOTTOM.
YOU GOTTA GIVE BEFORE
YOU TAKE.
WAH, WAH,
WAH-OO, WAH-OO,

TOMORROW YOU JUST
MIGHT
GET A BREAK.

EVERYBODY – *(etc.)*

AHHH –

EVERYBODY STARTS AT
THE BOTTOM.
NOBODY IS BORN A STAR.
EVERY DAY YOU GOTTA
FIND A WAY
TO SHOW THEM WHO
YOU ARE.

ALEXIS, DEEDEE & BIANCA.

EVERYBODY STARTS AT THE BOTTOM.

YOU GOTTA GIVE BEFORE YOU TAKE.

DON'T LOSE SIGHT OF WHAT YOU DREAM TONIGHT.

DEEDEE.

TOMORROW YOU JUST MIGHT –

BIANCA.

TOMORROW YOU JUST MIGHT –

ALEXIS.

TOMORROW YOU JUST MIGHT –

ALEXIS, DEEDEE & BIANCA.

GET A BREAK!

(Blackout)

#6-A: Gallery of Ghouls #2

(After the applause, we hear the 78 r.p.m. recording and the Queen's scuffling feet in the dark. The special lights come up, revealing **TONYA** *holding a large movie poster for "Attack of the Fifty Foot Woman." She pulls it away to reveal* **NADINE** *dressed as Allison Hayes in the same pose, wearing a strapless bra and miniskirt made from a white bed sheet and holding a small toy car. The lights fade out, the* **QUEENS** *scuffle off in the dark and the music ends. After a beat, the stage lights come up and* **BIANCA** *runs on, carrying a piece of paper. She now wears a bright gingham dress which she is quickly zipping and buttoning. She pushes the "stop" button on the boom box, gasping for air.)*

BIANCA. Wooo! That was quick! Oh, my –

(more primping and adjusting)

Is everything tucked in alright? I swear, that one gets faster every night. Now then – here's a fan letter addressed to me!

(squints to read, then reluctantly pulls eyeglasses from cleavage and puts them on)

Please let's just keep this to ourselves. I am not especially proud of my little deficiency.

(reads)

"Dear Bianca: I am a high school drama student from Cowcreek, Kentucky, and am totally your biggest fan. But how come I never see pictures of you and your family rolling around in the backyard like in *People* magazine?"

(smiles, puts the eyeglasses and the piece of paper back into her cleavage.)

Isn't that sweet! Well, my movie life I share with the fans, but my private life is my own. The spotlight only shines on me. Joe Bob and our two boys encourage my career, but the rest of the family – especially Momma and Poppa back in Arkansas – well, they never really understood what I do, and why. I had a very strict religious upbringing in a little town in the middle of nowhere.

(pushes the "play" button on the boom box and the music begins)

SONG #7: "I'M ALRIGHT, MOMMA"

We wrote letters back and forth for years, trying to bridge the gap.

(mimes writing)

"Dear Momma and Poppa –"
  WHEN I ASKED TO LEAVE THE FARM
  YOU TOLD ME TALES ABOUT THE HARM
  THAT COMES TO YOUNG GIRLS LIVIN' IN THE CITY.
  BUT I THUMBED MY WAY DOWN COUNTRY ROUTES
  AND USED MY NAT'RAL ATTRIBUTES
  TO GET TO WHERE I NOW AM SITTIN' PRETTY.
  I'M WORKIN' IN THE MOVIES.
  IT'S A LOT MORE FUN THAN FARMIN'.
  WHO'DA THOUGHT THAT I'D TURN OUT SO WELL.
  SO STOP ALL OF YER FRETTIN'.
  YOU BOTH A-KEEP FERGETTIN'
  YER LITTLE BABY GIRL AIN'T GOIN' TO HELL.

AND I'M ALRIGHT, MOMMA.
I'M HAPPIER NOW THAN I HAVE EVER BEEN.
AND I'M ALRIGHT. POPPA.
'CAUSE ACTIN' IN A MOVIN' "PITCHER"
IS A GOOD WAY TO GET RICHER,
AND SINCE IT AIN'T IN THE SCRIPTURE
DON'T KEEP CALLIN' IT A SIN.

(short dance break)

MOTHERS LIKE TO GET UPSET
ABOUT THE CHILDREN THEY BEGET.
IT GIVES 'EM SOMETHIN' MORE TO DO THAN
COOKIN'.
OH, YOU WORRY 'BOUT THE PATH WE TAKE
BUT, MA, YOU NEEDN'T LIE AWAKE,
ESPECIALLY WHEN YER DAUGHTER'S SO GOOD-
LOOKIN'.

MY HUSBAND AND MY KIDS ARE GREAT
AND I AM SORTA FAMOUS,
AND WE GOT A HOUSE UP ON A HILL.
SO STOP ALL YER COMPLAININ'.
I AIN'T IN THE LAND OF CANAAN.
I'M IN THE LAND OF CECIL B. DEMILLE.

(gestures like Charlton Heston as Moses)

AND I'M ALRIGHT, MOMMA.
JOE BOB AND BOTH THE TWINS ARE EATIN' GOOD.
AND I'M ALRIGHT, POPPA.
THE WORK IS EASY AND IT'S STEADY
AND I'VE SAVED ENOUGH ALREADY
TO HAVE BOTH OF YOU COME VISIT US
SOMEDAY IN HOLLYWOOD.

*(**NADINE** enters as "MA" wearing an old bonnet and apron and carrying a small Bible, followed by **TONYA** as "PA" wearing a straw hat, overalls, fake beard and carrying a pitchfork. They pose like "American Gothic.")*

NADINE.

OUR BELOVED DEAREST DAUGHTER,
ME AN' PA DON'T THINK WE OUGHTA
GO TO HOLLYWOOD AND VISIT – DO WE?

(nudges **TONYA***)*

TONYA. Nope.

NADINE.

YOU KNOW TRAV'LIN' DON'T AGREE WITH US.
THE FURTHEST WE HAVE BEEN BY BUS
WAS A COUNTY FAIR JUST OUTSIDE OF ST. LOUIE.

(nudges **TONYA***)*

TONYA. Yep.

NADINE.

AWAY OUT THERE WITH ALL THOSE SINNERS
YOU ARE PLAYIN' WITH FIRE.
THE DEVIL WILL GRAB YOU BY YER PURTY NECK.
HE KNOWS WHAT YOU BEEN UP TO.
HE KNOWS HOW TO CORRUPT YOU.

TONYA.

BUT BY THE WAY, WE THANK YOU FOR THE CHECK!

(pulls check from cleavage, winks to audience and **NADINE***, puts it back)*

NADINE.

WELL, IT'S –

NADINE & TONYA.

ALRIGHT, BIANCA.

NADINE.

THE RIGHTEOUS ROAD IS NOT FER ALL TO TREAD.
BUT IT'S –

NADINE & TONYA.

ALRIGHT, BIANCA.

TONYA.

TO FIND YER HAPPINESS AND LAUGHTER,
YER JIST DOIN' WHAT YOU HAVE TA.
WE'LL MEET UP IN THE HEREAFTA
AND SEE WHO COMES OUT AHEAD.

OPTION: WITHOUT INTERMISSION

BIANCA.	NADINE & TONYA.
WELL, I'M ALRIGHT, MOMMA.	WELL, IT'S ALRIGHT, BIANCA.
THE RIGHTEOUS ROAD IS NOT FER ALL TO TREAD.	THE RIGHTEOUS ROAD IS NOT FER ALL TO TREAD.
BUT I'M ALRIGHT, POPPA.	BUT IT'S ALRIGHT, BIANCA.
TO FIND MY HAPPINESS AND LAUGHTER	TO FIND YER HAPPINESS AND LAUGHTER
I'M JIST DOIN' WHAT I HAVETA.	YER JIST DOIN' WHAT YOU HAVETA.
WE'LL MEET UP IN THE HEREAFTA	WE'LL MEET UP IN THE HEREAFTA
AND SEE WHO – COMES – OUT – AHEAD –	AND SEE WHO – COMES – OUT – AHEAD –
YEE-HAH!	YEE-HAH!

(After the applause, **BIANCA**, **TONYA** *and* **NADINE** *exit as* **ALEXIS** *enters from the opposite side and pushes the "stop" button on the boom box.)*

CONTINUE TO PAGE 42

OPTION: WITH INTERMISSION

(**RICHELLE**, **ALEXIS** *and* **DEEDEE**, *also dressed as country farm girls enter and join* **NADINE** *and* **TONYA**.)

BIANCA.	OTHERS.
WELL, I'M ALRIGHT, MOMMA.	WELL, IT'S ALRIGHT, BIANCA.
THE RIGHTEOUS ROAD IS NOT FER ALL TO TREAD.	THE RIGHTEOUS ROAD IS NOT FER ALL TO TREAD.
BUT I'M ALRIGHT, POPPA.	BUT IT'S ALRIGHT, BIANCA.
TO FIND MY HAPPINESS AND LAUGHTER	TO FIND YER HAPPINESS AND LAUGHTER
I'M JIST DOIN' WHAT I HAVETA.	YER JIST DOIN' WHAT YOU HAVETA.
WE'LL MEET UP IN THE HEREAFTA	WE'LL MEET UP IN THE HEREAFTA
AND SEE WHO – COMES – OUT – AHEAD –	AND SEE WHO – COMES – OUT – AHEAD –
YEE-HAH!	YEE-HAH!

(Blackout)

End of Act I

ACT TWO

#7-A: ENTR'ACTE

(When the Entr'acte concludes and the house lights dim, the stage lights fade up and **ALEXIS** *enters, pushes the "stop" button on the boom box and ad-libs greetings to the audience.)*

CONTINUE TO PAGE 42

ALEXIS. The question I get most often is: "What's a nice girl like you with a Ph.D doing in a place like this?" Hey, in my neighborhood, fat girls HAD to be smart or they got married before they were seventeen and ended-up in a fourth floor waterfront flat facing New Jersey. Don't ask me why, but the harder I worked shrinking my ass and my thighs, the easier it was expanding my brain. College, grad school, summa cum laude. But when I realized I had $80,000 in college loans to pay off that's when I started using my brain to write and produce my own horror videos. Which reminds me – tomorrow they're showing one of our better movies here: "Revenge of the Psycho Bimbos." We made this one right around the time a whole slew of "living dead" movies came out. We agreed to do it for the kick of working together and because we were supposed to shoot right near where I live in the Hollywood Hills.

(pushes the "play" button on the boom box and the music begins)

SONG #8: "SOUTH OF THE BORDER"

Well, surprise, surprise – there was a last minute emergency and I remember having to call up the girls in the middle of the night with the bad news.

(The lights change and the **OTHERS** *enter wearing large sombreros and serapes.)*

WE'RE GONNA SHOOT SOUTH OF THE BORDER.
WE'RE DRIVING DOWN TO MEXICO.
BE SURE YOUR PASSPORTS ARE IN ORDER
AND SEE THE DOCTOR BEFORE WE GO.

THERE IS THE VAN, SO GET ABOARD HER.
WE GOT A THOUSAND MILES TO GO.
WE'RE GONNA SHOOT SOUTH OF THE BORDER
AND WE ARE DRIVING DOWN TO MEXICO.

(short dance break)

WE HAVE TO FLEE
FROM THE UNIONS IN HOLLYWOOD.
THEY COULD STOP PRODUCTION FOR GOOD.
IF THEY CAUGHT US FILMING, THEY WOULD.

WE'RE PAID IN CASH.
YOU CAN TAKE YOUR TEN NINETY-NINES,
SHOVE 'EM WHERE THE SUN NEVER SHINES.
AT LEAST WE AREN'T IN UNEMPLOYMENT LINES.

MAMA, YO QUIERO,
MAMA, YO QUIERO,
MAMA, YO QUIERO TO BE MAKING THE DINERO.

WE'RE GONNA SHOOT SOUTH OF THE BORDER.
WE'RE DRIVING DOWN TO MEXICO.
THE SETS ARE CHEAP AND MADE TO ORDER
AT THIS DESERTED LITTLE STUDIO.

*(**ALEXIS** hides behind the **OTHERS** and gets a few costume pieces from underneath the table.)*

OTHERS.

THEY BROUGHT A DIGITAL CAMCORDER
SO WE GO STRAIGHT TO VIDEO.
WE'RE GONNA SHOOT SOUTH OF THE BORDER
AND WE ARE DRIVING DOWN TO MEXICO.

*(As the **OTHERS** mime driving in an old rickety van, **ALEXIS** appears as "Carmen Miranda.")*

ALEXIS.   **OTHERS.**

YI, YI, YI, YI, YI, YI, YI,
I YI-YI-YI-YI DON'T LIKE IT VERY
MUCH,
SHOO-SHOO-SHOO-SHOO
SHOOTING ON THE RUN.
EVERY MOVIE THIS DIRECTOR EVER
TOUCHES
ENDS UP NEVER BEING SEEN BY
ANYONE.

I YI-YI-YI-YI DO NOT THINK IT IS FAIR	I YI-YI-YI-YI-YI-YI,
WAY-WAY-WAY-WAY OUT HERE WITH	BOOM, BOOM, BOOM,
THESE MEN.	BOOM, CHICKY
EVERY SCENE I'M RUNNING IN MY	*(etc.)*
UNDERWEAR	
AND THEN THE CREW SAYS I	
SHOULD DO IT ONCE AGAIN.	

(The music underscores as they all move downstage.)

ALEXIS. But what zombie movie would be complete without armies of the living dead chewing up the countryside? Shooting on location is hell for us, but it's great for all the locals who get to be extras! And we're scouting for some extras right now!

(The **QUEENS** *select a few people from the audience, bring them to the front of the stage and dress them in the sombreros and serapes.)*

How many of you have seen "Night of the Living Dead?"

(play the response)

Have ever seen a "living dead" movie?

(play the response)

Are actually "living dead" after being at this convention all day?

(play the response)

Now, my little extras, in the climax of this scene, the ghouls are surrounding us in the deserted farmhouse. And this is how a ghoul chases a scream queen.

(SEE AUTHOR'S NOTES: "BORDER" VIDEO)

(The **QUEENS** *teach the extras how to walk like zombies and moan "brains.")*

Ready? Action!!

*(***ALEXIS*** *slaps a movie clapboard and the* **QUEENS** *coax the "ghouls" to chase them in front of the stage.)*

Cut! That was great!!

*(***ALEXIS*** *leads the audience applause as the* **QUEENS** *take back the sombreros and serapes and escort the extras back to their seats; then,)*

WE SHOOT AT DAWN
JUST AS SOON AS THERE'S ENOUGH LIGHT.
BUT IF SOMETHING DOESN'T GO RIGHT
WE'LL KEEP SHOOTING ALL THROUGH THE NIGHT.

AND WE ARE FED
EVERY DAY RIGHT THERE ON THE SET.
HAVEN'T GOT FOOD POISONING YET.
BUT FOR ALL OF THIS GRIEF, JUST WHAT DO I GET?

MAMA, YO QUIERO,
MAMA, YO QUIERO,
MAMA, YO QUIERO TO BE DRIVING A CAMARO!

(They mime driving home in their rickety van.)

ALL.

BUT THERE'S THE VAN, SO GET ABOARD HER.
WE GOT A THOUSAND MILES TO GO.
IT IS A WRAP SOUTH OF THE BORDER
AND WE ARE DRIVING HOME FROM MEXICO –.

(Blackout)

*(After the applause, the **OTHERS** exit and the lights fade up on **RICHELLE**. She pushes the "stop" button on the boom box.)*

RICHELLE. That trip was a real blast. And the video was a big seller in Malaysia or somewhere, I think. We have fans all over the world; Near East, Far East, Middle East. Somehow bootleg copies of our videos find their way into the skankiest places! I heard from one soldier boy how he single-handedly captured a whole house full of rebels during Desert Storm because they were huddled around a tiny portable T.V. watching "Malibu Vampire Vixens." You hear that, Spike Spiegleman? World Peace, direct-to-video, thanks to the Scream Queens. I don't mind the label "Scream Queen" but it sorta gets in the way when you try to have a real life. I was always choosy about the guys I'd go out with. But bigger cars meant bigger egos, and they were usually just the same generic losers.

(pushes the "play" button on the boom box and the music begins)

SONG #9: "HAPPY ENDINGS"

I guess that's the price of my stardom – playing the same character in one sequel after another.

IN STORIES I GREW UP WITH
AND MOVIES I'VE SEEN SINCE
THE GIRL WHO WAITS THE LONGEST
GETS MARRIED TO THE PRINCE.
THEY ALWAYS HAVE THEIR HAPPY ENDINGS;
FADE OUTS AND HAPPY ENDINGS.
BUT THAT'S NOT HOW IT WORKS FOR ME.

WHENEVER GUYS APPROACH ME
THEY SEE THE MOVIE STAR;
THE GIRL WHO'S USUALLY NAKED
INSIDE THEIR V.C.R.
IT NEVER LEADS TO HAPPY ENDINGS;
SUNSETS AND HAPPY ENDINGS.
THAT KIND OF STUFF AIN'T MEANT FOR ME.

SO MANY MEN SAY THEY WANT ME.
SO MANY MEN SAY THEY CARE.
BUT WHEN THEY SEE ME WAKE UP WITHOUT MY MAKE-UP,
AND CURLERS IN MY HAIR – THEY STARE.

THAT ACTRESS IN THE POSTER,
SHE'S NOT THE REAL ME.
BUT THAT'S WHAT EVERY BOYFRIEND
EXPECTS THAT I SHOULD BE.
SO HOW THE HELL CAN HAPPY ENDINGS,
HEART-WARMING HAPPY ENDINGS,
ONES THAT SEEM TOO GOOD TO BE TRUE,
BE MINE – WHEN THIS IS ALL I DO?

SO HOW THE HELL CAN HAPPY ENDINGS,
HEART-WARMING HAPPY ENDINGS,
ONES THAT SEEM TOO GOOD TO BE TRUE,
BE MINE – WHEN THIS IS ALL I DO? –

(lights fade out)

(After the applause, the stage lights return to normal. **RICHELLE** *has exited and* **DEEDEE** *enters. She pushes*

the "stop" button on the boom box and holds up a small piece of paper.)

DEEDEE. Hey, we just got this message from the chauffeur at the airport and our Lifetime Achievement Award winner should be here any minute. And all kidding aside – Spike Spiegleman, if you're still out there – that little joke I made earlier about blowing you for an audition –

(chuckles, looks around, then seriously)

– still goes! As most of you know, I'm the only one up here who is a California native. It was a pretty dull, normal childhood for me. By normal, I mean I thought everyone lived in a high desert trailer park. We got lousy TV reception and my parents didn't read, so I never imagined there was a whole different world down there in the L.A. basin. When I dropped out of Dusty Springs High School and "negotiated" a ride to Venice beach, I finally got an apartment. My own apartment! It was the first time I slept in a room that wasn't up on concrete blocks. A boy who lived in the building had a Super 8 camera and begged me to star in his little home-made monster movies. Since then, I've hardly ever turned down an acting job. This is the stuff they said I CAN show here.

DEEDEE'S DEMO REEL: *(see author's notes)*

(The stage lights fade out and the video screen lights up with clips from some of her non-porno films. After the last clip, the screen goes dark and the stage lights return to normal.)

Well, there you have it. I can think of worse ways to make a living, and believe me – I've probably done it.

*(The **OTHERS** enter as the house lights fade up over the crowd.)*

RICHELLE. But now it's your turn. We've been telling you what we THINK you wanna know about us. Let's find out what's really on your minds.

(**NOTE:** *This can be completely improvised if the actresses are adept at fielding cold questions from the audience, or the audience can fill out index cards with their questions about the Queens before the show and during intermission. The cards can be screened in advance for questions that will permit the actresses to improvise the most entertaining answers.* **RICHELLE** *can read the cards and direct the questions to the appropriate Scream Queen. This Q&A session should only last long enough to get a few strong laughs; two or three minutes at most.*)

(**RICHELLE,** *or an audience plant, directs the final question to* **DEEDEE.**)

RICHELLE. *(cont.)* DeeDee, what's the most important thing about being a successful Scream Queen?

(**ALEXIS** *pushes the "play" button on the boom box and the music begins.*)

SONG #10: "DON'T OPEN THAT DOOR"

DEEDEE. That's for me? Well, I'll tell ya –
AFTER A YEAR IN THIS BUSINESS,
I GUESS I KNEW IT ALL,
'CAUSE IN THIS BUSINESS
THERE AIN'T VERY MUCH TO KNOW.
SHOW UP ON TIME AND STAY IN SHAPE
AND ALWAYS LICK YOUR LIPS.
BUT I'D LIKE TO PASS ALONG A FEW MORE TIPS.

EVERY BABYSITTER WHO IS HOME ALONE FOR THE FIRST TIME
HATES TO HEAR THOSE FUNNY LITTLE NOISES IN THE HOUSE.
WHAT'S THAT CREAKING IN THE ATTIC?
WHAT'S THAT SQUEAKING ON THE STAIR?
SHOULD SHE GET OFF THE SOFA AND SEE WHAT THE HELL IS THERE?

MY ADVICE TO HER WOULD BE TO JUST COMPLETELY IGNORE IT.
I HAVE DONE THE SCENE MORE THAN ONCE OR

TWICE BEFORE.
IF YOU WANT TO LIVE 'TIL MORNING
DON'T BE BRAVE AND DON'T EXPLORE.
AND DON'T GO INTO THAT NURSERY,
AND DON'T ANSWER THAT TELEPHONE,
AND DON'T, DON'T –

(sound of "knock, knock")

DON'T OPEN THAT DOOR.

(short musical break where spooky lights and sounds scare her; the **OTHERS** *exit)*

YOU CAN BET WHENEVER THERE'S A WOMAN
TAKING A SHOWER
THERE'S A PSYCHO LURKING IN THE SHADOWS
SOMEWHERE NEAR.
HE WILL POP OUT OF THE CLOSET
OR HE'LL BREAK A WINDOW PANE.
IF YOU'RE LUCKY HE'LL BE TONY PERKINS OR
MICHAEL CAINE.

THERE ARE CERTAIN THINGS A MOVIE ACTRESS HAS
TO REMEMBER
IF SHE DOESN'T WANT TO BE DEAD MEAT ON THE
FLOOR.
IF YOU'D LIKE TO DO THE SEQUEL
AND AVOID MOST OF THE GORE,
JUST DON'T GO INTO THAT NURSERY
AND DON'T ANSWER THAT TELEPHONE,
AND DON'T, DON'T –

(sound of "knock, knock")

DON'T OPEN THAT DOOR.

(Dance break; The **OTHERS** *enter wearing Halloween masks and stand in a line facing away from the audience. One at a time,* **DEEDEE** *mimes knocking on a door next to them and they turn around and scare her. The last mask should be a known non-horror character, like an unpopular politician or celebrity from the late 1990s, which scares* **DEEDEE** *the most.)*

OTHERS.   DEEDEE.

NEVER, NEVER FORGET TO
TURN ON THE OUTSIDE
LIGHT.
NEVER, NEVER FORGET TO
LOCK ALL THE WINDOWS
TIGHT.
NEVER FORGET TO KEEP
YOUR FLASHLIGHT
READY AT YOUR SIDE BY THE
T.V. GUIDE.
NEVER FORGET THAT IT'S
NOT SAFE TO
RUN AROUND AND PLAY IN A
NEGLIGEE.

NEVER, NEVER FORGET THAT   THERE ARE CERTAIN THINGS
YOU CAN DIAL 9-1-1.   A MOVIE ACTRESS
NEVER, NEVER FORGET THEY   HAS TO REMEMBER
LOVE IT WHEN YOU SCREAM   IF SHE DOESN'T WANT TO BE
AND RUN.   DEAD MEAT ON THE FLOOR.
                              IF YOU'D –

ALL.

LIKE TO DO THE SEQUEL
AND AVOID MOST OF THE GORE,
JUST DON'T GO INTO THAT NURSERY
AND DON'T ANSWER THAT TELEPHONE,
AND DON'T, DON'T –

(sound of "knock, knock")

DON'T OPEN THAT DOOR.

EVEN THOUGH WE KNOW HOW TO DEFEAT A SERIAL
KILLER
WE DON'T EVER GET A CHANCE TO PRACTICE WHAT
WE PREACH.
IF THE BIMBOS IN B-MOVIES NEVER MET A GRISLY END,
WHAT'S THE POINT, WHERE'S THE FUN, AND WHY
WOULD ANYONE ATTEND?

(They form a kick line.)

SO WE DO THE STUPID THINGS THAT ALWAYS PUT
US IN DANGER.

THAT IS WHAT A HORROR FILM HEROINE IS FOR.

DEEDEE.

AND WE KNOW HOW WHEN YOU WATCH US
HOW YOU SECRETLY IMPLORE:

ALL.

HEY, DON'T GO INTO THAT NURSERY
AND DON'T ANSWER THAT TELEPHONE
AND DON'T REACH FOR THAT CARVING KNIFE

DEEDEE. And don't even THINK about takin' a shit!

ALL.

AND DON'T, DON'T, DON'T, DON'T, DON'T, DON'T

(sound of "knock, knock")

DON'T OPEN THAT DOOR –

Don't open that door! Oooo!

(Blackout)

#10-A: Gallery of Ghouls #3

(After the applause, the 78 r.p.m. recording plays, the **QUEENS** *scuffle into their places, and the special lights come up to reveal* **TONYA** *holding a large black and white photo blow-up of Janet Leigh screaming in the "Psycho" shower scene.* **TONYA** *pulls the photo away revealing* **RICHELLE** *wrapped in a clear plastic shower curtain, frozen in the same pose.* **TONYA** *squirts* **RICHELLE** *with a spray bottle full of water as the lights fade out, the* **QUEENS** *scuffle off and the music ends.)*

(As the stage lights return to normal, the cell phone is heard ringing again. **DEEDEE**, **NADINE**, **BIANCA** *and* **ALEXIS** *run in and grab the cell phones from their bags.)*

ALL. *(perky, professional voices)* Hello?

BIANCA. Mine. Excuse me.

(The **OTHERS** *put their phones back in the bags as* **ALEXIS** *pushes the "stop" button on the boom box and* **BIANCA** *talks into the phone.)*

Cletus, Mommy told you this number is only for emergencies. What emergency? If Daddy says it's time for bed, you move your little buns into that bed! No, Mommy, can't sing you to sleep. We're in the middle of a show here!

(holds phone up to audience)

I've got a five-year-old with a mind of his own. Can you folks help me out with his favorite lullaby?

*(**BIANCA** and the **OTHERS** sing gently, coaxing the audience to join in.)*

ALL.

"The worms crawl in, the worms crawl out.

The worms play pinochle on your snout.

They eat your eyes, they eat your hat,

They crawl in skinny and crawl out fat."

BIANCA. *(motherly sigh)* Goodnight, sweetheart. Sleep tight.

(puts phone in bag, turns to audience)

Thank you so much.

*(**RICHELLE** enters, waving a small piece of paper.)*

RICHELLE. They just handed me this piece of paper backstage. Our mystery celebrity guest wasn't even on the plane. We've been stood-up!

*(The **OTHERS** moan.)*

NADINE. But we made all these plans!

BIANCA. And rehearsed the number!

ALEXIS. Hollywood creep! But we should tell them who it was anyway.

RICHELLE. Ladies and gentlemen – this year's GlamaGore ScreamiCon Lifetime Achievement Award winner is – was – Mr. Roger Corman!

#10-B: FANFARE

*(The **OTHERS** lead the audience applause as **TONYA** enters with a life-sized cardboard stand-up of a smiling Roger Corman.)*

TONYA. We had this made-up, just in case.

RICHELLE. *(speaks to the stand-up)* Mr. Corman – for all of the memorable movies you've churned out over the past fifty years – and for the level of excellence in filmmaking to which you constantly aspired – and sometimes found – the Scream Queens proudly present you with –

(looks impatiently at **DEEDEE***)*

*(***DEEDEE** *quickly rummages through her bag, pulling out various personal items, finally revealing a small trophy that looks like it was found at a thrift store, and hands it ceremoniously to* **RICHELLE***.)*

– with this Lifetime Achievement Award.

(The **QUEENS** *applaud.)*

We'll deliver this to his office on Monday.

TONYA. Corman was a major influence on all our careers –

NADINE. – and everyone else's.

ALEXIS. He once gave a lecture for the film students at my college. The next day, you couldn't find a roll of Super 8 anywhere in the neighborhood.

RICHELLE. He made the whole world realize that you could actually produce a feature-length movie and make a profit using a minimum of talent –

TONYA. – and time –

NADINE. – and money –

RICHELLE. – and production values –

NADINE. – and money!

BIANCA. He was never like that with me.

NADINE. You worked with Roger Corman?

BIANCA. Well, not worked with. But we did lunch three times a week.

(pushes the "play" button on the boom box and the music begins)

SONG #11: "ROGER CORMAN"

BIANCA.

> I WAS A WAITRESS AT THE DELI
> AND I SERVED EVERY HOLLYWOOD EXEC.
> SOME WERE CRUDE, SOME WERE CRASS,
> SOME WOULD GRAB MY ASS.
> BUT THERE'S ONLY ONE WHO NEVER TRIED TO
> SKIP OUT ON THE CHECK.

(The **OTHERS** *put on wrap-around poodle skirts and form a 50s doo-wop back-up group behind* **BIANCA***; see vocal score.)*

MAYBE HE'S STINGY, MAYBE HE'S CHEAP.
HIS MOVIES CAN EXCITE YOU OR PUT YOU TO SLEEP.
BUT ROGER CORMAN ALWAYS LEFT A BIG TIP FOR
ME.

HE NEVER SPLURGES, HE NEVER SPENDS
EXCEPT WHEN HE WANTS A NEW MERCEDES BENZ.
BUT ROGER CORMAN ALWAYS LEFT A BIG TIP FOR
ME.

> HE'LL NEVER WASTE A SINGLE DOLLAR
> UNTIL HE'S GOT THE MOST FROM EVERY DIME.
> AND YOU WILL NEVER HEAR HIM HOLLER:
> "LET'S DO THAT SCENE JUST ONE MORE TIME!"

STILL HE'S A LEGEND; STILL, HE'S UNIQUE.
HE'LL SHOOT ONE OR TWO MOVIES IN LESS THAN A
WEEK.
BUT ROGER CORMAN ALWAYS LEFT A BIG TIP FOR,
TWENTY-FIVE PER CENT FOR,
LEFT A BIG TIP FOR ME.

(The **OTHERS** *continue humming as the video screen lights up with a montage of clips from public domain trailers featuring some of Corman's most laughable, low-budget monsters.)*

ROGER CORMAN ALWAYS LEFT A BIG TIP FOR ME.
ROGER CORMAN ALWAYS LEFT A BIG TIP FOR ME.

(The montage ends with a clip of **BIANCA** *as a waitress*

*in a restaurant and a man whose face is unseen giving
her money and goosing her as he steps out of frame.)*

AND ROGER HAS THE REPUTATION
OF ASKING EVERYONE TO WORK FOR FREE.
AND YET THE KING OF EXPLOITATION
NEVER ONCE EXPLOITED ME.

BABY, BABY, BABY,
HE IS THE GENIUS, HE'S THE AUTEUR.
HIS FILMS WILL LIVE FOREVER AS CLASSICS –

OTHERS. For sure!

ALL.

ROGER CORMAN, THAT PENNY-PINCHING S.O.B.
WE REALLY LOVE YA,
DONTCHA KNOW WE LOVE YA,

BIANCA.

'CAUSE HE ALWAYS LEFT A BIG FAT

ALL.

TIP FOR ME –!

*(The **QUEENS** huddle together around the stand-up for
a cheesecake pose.)*

BIANCA. We're ready for our close-up, Mr. Corman.

*(On the last note, a photo flash from above captures their
tableau.)*

*(After the applause, **DEEDEE**, **TONYA** and **NADINE** exit
with the trophy and the stand-up. **RICHELLE** pushes the
"stop" button on the boom box and moves downstage
with **BIANCA** and **ALEXIS**.)*

RICHELLE. Listen up, Spike! There's one horror film magazine – whose name I will not mention – that once
labeled us "The Three Stooges" of slasher movies.

BIANCA. I don't get it.

ALEXIS. I guess because we co-star so often together as a
team.

RICHELLE. And because we hit each other with deadly hand
tools and poke each other's eyes out.

ALEXIS. Ah, yes.

BIANCA. Anyway, our friendship goes back quite a ways. I first met Richelle at a gym off Sunset Boulevard.

ALEXIS. I met her at an Adult Ed. Art class at UCLA. I was the young sculptor – she was the naked model.

RICHELLE. You can't imagine what I did for money back then. We hung out together, making the audition rounds and I was the first one to land a few small supporting parts.

ALEXIS. A corpse here, a cadaver there –

RICHELLE. One day I brought the girls out to a location shoot and Teddy Ray Olsen put us in our first scene together – "Full Moon Slumber Party."

RICHELLE, ALEXIS & BIANCA'S DEMO REEL: *(see author's notes)*

(The stage lights dim as the video screen lights up with scenes featuring the three friends. After the last clip, the video screen goes dark, the stage lights return to normal, the three **QUEENS** *share a sentimental beat and a group hug.* **DEEDEE**, **NADINE** *and* **TONYA** *enter.)*

NADINE. OK, Spike, dahling. I had my agent fax me the casting breakdown on this new film of yours.

(reads fax)

"Rhonda; early thirties, attractive, sincere, good screamer, nudity required. MaryAnn; late twenties, attractive, shy, blonde, vulnerable, nudity required. Consuela; thirties, attractive, hardened ex-con, lots of nudity required."

(to audience)

And the list goes on and on! And they're all within my age range, for God's sake! What are you waiting for?

(reads fax)

"All roles require extensive use of special make-up effects."

BIANCA. Ahh, the make-up effects. Now that's probably the MOST humiliating thing a Scream Queen has to put up with.

NADINE. That, and everyone walking past your table at an autograph show.

RICHELLE. The gory make-up tricks are what make our movies special!

ALEXIS. They're gross.

DEEDEE. They're sticky.

RICHELLE. They sell tickets!

*(The **OTHERS** quickly unpack the make-up props from their bags as **RICHELLE** pushes the "play" button on the boom box and the music begins.)*

SONG #12: "SPECIAL FX"

RICHELLE.

BIG PRODUCERS WHO SIGN ALL THE CHECKS
SEEM TO KNOW WHAT THE PUBLIC EXPECTS.
HUGE EXPLOSIONS AND MUSCULAR BRAWLERS
AND MILLIONS OF DOLLARS IN SPECIAL FX.

HELPLESS VICTIMS A DOCTOR DISSECTS,
FLYING DEMONS A WITCH RESURRECTS.
SPACE INVADERS WHO LOOK AWFULLY HEINOUS
LIKE THEY'RE FROM URANUS, ARE SPECIAL FX.

BIANCA.

AND EVEN IN THE LITTLE NO-BUDGET FILMS THAT WE DO,
A COUPLE GUYS KNOW HOW TO MAKE OUR BLOOD SPRAY, SPURT AND SPEW.

RICHELLE.

THAT'S WHAT THE FANS PAY TO SEE,
SO IF THEY LOVE IT, WE'LL GIVE 'EM MORE OF IT.

NADINE.

WHEN A VAMPIRE DROPS BY AND INJECTS
BOTH HIS CANINES DEEP INTO OUR NECKS,

DEEDEE.

THOUGH IT LOOKS LIKE A REAL TRANSFUSION,
IT'S JUST THE ILLUSION

ALL.

OF SPECIAL FX.

(Music underscores as the **QUEENS** *demonstrate the various gory props and make-up effects: knife slitting a throat, hatchet in the head, sliced veins, fake vomit, etc. As* **BIANCA** *and* **NADINE** *enact a girl fight at one side,)*

TONYA.

NEARLY EACH FILM DE PALMA DIRECTS
HAS AN EXCESS OF VIOLENCE AND SEX.
BRUTAL FIGHT SCENES THAT PULL ALL THE STOPS
OUT.
IF SOMEONE'S EYE POPS OUT –

*(***BIANCA'***s eye "pops out.")*

– THAT'S SPECIAL FX.

*(***ALEXIS** *steps forward wearing a specially-rigged male chest piece, sunglasses and a leather jacket.)*

RICHELLE.

WHEN JAMES CAMERON YELLS DOWN TO THE
TECHS,
"I WANT MORE BLOOD ON SCHWARZ'NEGGER'S
PECS!"
THEN THE WHOLE CREW IS FRANTICALLY RUSHING
'TIL ARNOLD IS GUSHING –

(Blood shoots out from **ALEXIS***' chest piece.)*

– WITH SPECIAL FX.

(Music underscores as more gore gags are demonstrated: playing catch with a severed head, juggling rubber hands and feet, spitting out rubber worms, entrails falling out, etc. They throw the props offstage, then,)

ALEXIS.

STEVEN SPIELBERG ONLY SELECTS
CERTAIN ACTORS WHOM HE RESPECTS.

DEEDEE.
YET THESE ACTORS WHOSE TALENT SO MATTERED
JUST USUALLY GET SPLATTERED

ALL.
BY SPECIAL FX.
WHEN YOU GO TO YOUR CINEMAPLEX
TO SEE CITIES A METEOR WRECKS,
JUST REMEMBER THAT WHAT YOU ARE SEEING
ALL CAME INTO BEING – THROUGH SPECIAL FX –.

(They pose with big smiles, vampire fangs and blood oozing from their mouths.)

(After the applause, ALEXIS pushes the "stop" button on the boom box.)

ALEXIS. Well, our time is up. That Polish wedding reception is waiting in the hall.

(sound of a door opening and accordion music coming from the back of the theater)

Hey!!

(sound of the door slamming shut)

We're not sticking around for that and neither should you.

RICHELLE. I'd like to make one last plea to Spike Spiegleman if he hasn't left for his screening yet.

BIANCA. As you saw here tonight, we still got it and we know how to use it.

TONYA. And we'd like to use it again before this new batch of teenage scream queens takes over the whole business.

NADINE. Well, dahlings, it happens. No matter how much you try to defy gravity, they always want them younger and firmer and higher.

DEEDEE. Which brings us to the final fan letter tonight from the mailbag.

(pulls letter from Neiman-Marcus bag and reads)

"Dear Queens: You've all given us so much joy throughout your productive careers. What will you do when it's time to retire?"

(The **QUEENS** *are speechless for a moment, then* **DEEDEE** *pushes the "play" button on the boom box and the music begins.)*

SONG #13: "REMEMBER THE NAME"

RICHELLE. Open an antique shop.

TONYA. Day care center.

NADINE. Acting school.

DEEDEE. Travel.

BIANCA. I'll be a grandmother.

ALEXIS. The important thing is if you keep clamoring for our movies, we won't HAVE to retire.

RICHELLE. But when we do, don't just throw us out with the recyclables. Please – I'm beggin' you –

REMEMBER THE NAME IF YOU SHOULD SEE ME.

RICHELLE & TONYA.

REMEMBER THE NAME AND WHO I WAS.

RICHELLE, TONYA & BIANCA.

REMEMBER THE NAME AND HOW YOU LOVED ME.
NO MATTER HOW TOMORROW FADES OUR MEMORIES
YOU'LL ALWAYS HAVE YOUR FANTASIES.
WE'LL HAVE OUR DOUBLE-"D"S.

ALL.

YOU CAN THINK OF US WHEN YOU'RE LONELY.
YOU CAN THINK OF US WHEN YOU'RE SAD.
BUT WHEN YOU THINK OF US, REMEMBER THE NAME
AND THE GOOD – TIMES THAT WE HAD.

DEEDEE.

REMEMBER THE NAME GOES WITH THE BODY.

DEEDEE & NADINE.

REMEMBER THE NAME IS WHAT WILL LAST.

DEEDEE, NADINE & ALEXIS.

REMEMBER THE NAME IS HOW YOU'LL FIND ME.
I'LL ALWAYS BE THERE FOR YOU, WITH OR WITHOUT CLOTHES,

AT LEAST UNTIL THE FILMS AND TAPES BEGIN TO
DECOMPOSE.

ALL.

YOU CAN THINK OF US WHEN YOU'RE LONELY.
YOU CAN THINK OF US WHEN YOU'RE SAD.
BUT WHEN YOU THINK OF US, REMEMBER THE
NAME
AND THE GOOD – TIMES THAT WE HAD.

SCREAM QUEENS MIGHT SAY GOOD-BYE,
BUT SCREAM QUEENS NEVER REALLY DIE.

ALEXIS.

WHEN YOU REMEMBER THE NAME AND DON'T
FORGET ME.

BIANCA.

REMEMBER THE NAME AFTER I'M GONE.

DEEDEE.

REMEMBER THE NAME WHEN THEY REPLACE ME.

RICHELLE.

CAREERS DON'T LAST FOREVER, NEW QUEENS WILL
WEAR THE CROWNS.

TONYA.

WE'LL PUT AWAY OUR SCRAPBOOKS,

NADINE.

AND WE'LL PUT ON FIFTY POUNDS.

ALL.

YOU CAN THINK OF US WHEN YOU'RE LONELY.
YOU CAN THINK OF US WHEN YOU'RE SAD.
BUT WHEN YOU THINK OF US, REMEMBER THE
NAME
AND THE GOOD – TIMES THAT WE HAD.

*(They march forward like Mouseketeers, picking up their
name cards from the table and holding them in front of
their chest.)*

TONYA. Tonya!

DEEDEE. DeeDee!

BIANCA. Bianca!

ALEXIS. Alexis!

RICHELLE. Richelle!

NADINE. *(really drunk by now)* Roy! I mean – Nadine!

ALL.

> SCREAM QUEENS MIGHT SAY GOOD-BYE,
> BUT SCREAM QUEENS NEVER REALLY DIE
>
> WHEN YOU REMEMBER THE NAME IF YOU SHOULD
> SEE ME.
> REMEMBER THE NAME AND WHO I WAS.
> REMEMBER THE NAME AND HOW YOU LOVED ME.
>
> NO MATTER HOW TOMORROW FADES OUR
> MEMORIES,
> YOU'LL ALWAYS HAVE YOUR FANTASIES.
> WE'LL HAVE OUR DOUBLE-"D"S.
>
> YOU CAN THINK OF US WHEN YOU'RE LONELY.
> YOU CAN THINK OF US WHEN YOU'RE SAD.
> BUT WHEN YOU THINK OF US, REMEMBER THE
> NAME
> AND THE GOOD – TIMES – THAT – WE –

> *(Just before the last note, the cell phone rings again. They freeze for a beat, not sure whether to sing the last note, then dive for the bags and pull out their phones.)*

> Hello?

RICHELLE. *(into phone)* Yes, it is! What?? Really? When??

> *(to* **OTHERS***)*

> It's Spike Spiegleman! He's so shy he's calling from the lobby. He caught the whole show from the back and wants to see all of us in Los Angeles on Monday morning!!

> *(They all scream and yell and jump around hysterically.)*

> ***SONG #14: "FINALE"***

ALL.

> THAT'S WHAT IT TAKES TO BE A SCREAM QUEEN.

(scream)

B-MOVIE BABES JUST MAKIN' A LIVING.
SCREAM QUEENS.

(scream)

SHAKIN' OUR TITS AND PAYIN' THE RENT.
STARE AT THIS HEAVING BUST,
ENVIOUS OR WITH LUST, THAT'S ALRIGHT.
BECAUSE WE'RE
SCREAM QUEENS, HERE ON EXHIBITION.
SCREAM QUEENS, FREE WITH THE ADMISSION.
YOU GOT TO SEE ALL YOUR FAV'RITE SCREAM
QUEENS
HERE – TONIGHT –.

(Blackout)

#14-A: CURTAIN CALL & EXIT MUSIC

End of Show

AUTHOR'S NOTES

Each "demo" is a series of original video clips supposedly from the actresses' movies; best screaming scenes, death scenes, dramatic scenes, or highlights from different films over the years, all played for laughs and spoofing the ridiculous cliches of the horror movie genre. Each demo should run approximately two minutes. Each actress narrates the clip as it appears on the video screen.

You may create these videos to suit your own creative talents, budgets and imaginations. The more outrageous and amateurish the clips are, the funnier they will be to watch.

The following "shooting script" from the original production can be shot as is, or simply used for inspiration.

TONYA'S DEMO REEL:

TONYA. This is from my first film, "The Texas MixMaster Massacre." The director still lived with his mother and I guess this was the scariest thing they had around the house.

(Dressed as a cheerleader, Tonya is chased by a psycho killer waving an electric mixer. Just as he corners her, the cord pops out of the wall socket, the mixer blades stop spinning, and **TONYA** *chases the killer into the woods.)*

And this is a scene from "Sorority House Bloodsuckers." I especially liked this one because I got to play a dual role.

(Dressed as a college coed in a fuzzy robe, **TONYA** *is in a bathroom brushing her teeth. A vampire hag, also played by* **TONYA** *in heavy make-up, appears and lunges for coed-***TONYA***'s throat. She takes a small crucifix off the wall, swats the hag, who screams and disappears.)*

And this, of course, you remember as "Revenge of the Barbarian Bitches." My years of cheerleader training came in very useful on this one.

(Dressed as a post-apocalyptic amazon in an animal-skin bikini, **TONYA** *is surrounded by several mutant grunts. She fights them off in stunning Bruce Lee-fashion, breaking arms and legs and skulls at random.)*

And finally, one of my all-time favorites – "Bimbo Babysitters." The director had this thing for Al Hitchcock and he figured, why not steal from the best?

(Imitating shot-for-shot the basement scene from "Psycho," **TONYA,** *dressed in a skimpy nightie, enters a dark storage room. An old lady in a grey wig and shawl sits motionless in a rocking chair with her back to the camera.* **TONYA** *touches her on the shoulder, spinning her around slowly and revealing a rotted corpse.* **TONYA** *screams and hits the hanging light behind her with her arm. The light shade hits* **TONYA** *in the head and she falls unconscious out of frame.)*

NADINE'S DEMO REEL:

NADINE. I began my career in television doing some modeling and then moving up into commercials.

(Recreating a 1950s black and white TV commercial, young **NADINE** *is dressed as the perfect little homemaker, cooking, cleaning and meal-planning.)*

I did a ton of extra work, then landed my first featured role in the British horror comedy, "Carry On Bleeding."

(Dressed as a comedic vampire, **NADINE** *chases a silly British couple through a haunted house. After a brief struggle, the woman pounds a wooden stake into* **NADINE***'s chest with blood gushing skyward.)*

This is a scene I still get asked about even after all these years. The salt and the butter and the oil oozed into every crack and crevice – but I did it in one take!

(Dressed as a movie theater usherette, **NADINE** *is trapped inside a large popcorn machine. As it heats up, lights flash, smoke and steam swirl around and the popcorn*

pops. **NADINE** *dies and falls face first into the mound of popcorn.)*

Oh, and this is from my latest film, "Attack of the Daylight Vampires." The producer was too cheap to rent the lighting equipment for the nighttime shots, so we changed the original title and created, I believe, an entirely new horror franchise.

*(Dressed in a leopard-skin bikini, **NADINE** is lounging poolside, sipping a martini. She gets buzzed by a rubber bat on a string and brushes it away. As a large shadow passes over her, we see the pool boy cleaning next to her. He suddenly sprouts fangs and pointy ears and moves towards her. **NADINE** screams, picks up two styrofoam swimming "noodles" next to her chair and holds them up like a crucifix. The pool boy melts and falls into the pool.)*

DEEDEE'S DEMO REEL:

DEEDEE. This is one of my early attempts at a straight horror film. It was kind of a stretch for me, acting-wise. It's called "Invasion of the Martian Furry Things." The director had a real fetish for "furry things" and found a dozen different ways to shoot up my skirt.

*(Dressed as a trashy hooker, **DEEDEE** is waiting on a street corner at night. Suddenly a "Martian Furry Thing" leaps out of the nearby bushes and goes for her throat. It's obviously an inanimate child's stuffed toy, but she wrestles with it, rolling around on the sidewalk while the camera POV tries to shoot up her skirt. **DEEDEE** picks up a shovel and kills the Furry Thing, then attacks the cameraman.)*

This film was a real boost for my career. I played the leader of this alien invasion force. You remember that old movie called "Mars Needs Women?" They called this one "Venus Needs Penis."

*(Dressed in a silver jumpsuit with a 50's beehive wig, **DEEDEE** enters a dark, fog-shrouded classroom and*

corners a teacher and several high school students. She eyes the bulging crotch of one of the jocks and pulls a ray gun from her belt. It's actually a large, round hole-boring drill that spins furiously as she approaches.)

Now this is the death scene that won me the Golden Schmeggegge *(pronounced: shmu-GAY-ghee)* Award a few years ago. It's called "Revenge of the Left-Handed Snake Breeders."

*(**DEEDEE** is relaxing with her eyes shut in a bubble bath, wearing nothing but a small pair of headphones connected to a CD player. An unseen killer opens the door and, with his left hand, drops a large snake into the tub. **DEEDEE** reacts slowly, then struggles hysterically and bloodily as the snake attacks and pulls her underwater, her foot kicking open the drain plug. When the water drains away, all that is left amongst the bubbles and blood is a skeleton wearing the headphones.)*

RICHELLE, ALEXIS & BIANCA'S DEMO REEL:

RICHELLE. It was obvious we worked good together, even from the beginning.

*(Dressed in flimsy nighties, the three **QUEENS** are having a teenage pajama party in front of a huge fireplace. As they share a big bowl of popcorn, **RICHELLE** pulls out a Ouija board and they huddle around it with their fingers on the planchette. After it slowly spells out "D-I-E," there's a flash of lightning and several nearby stuffed animals leap onto the **QUEENS** and maul them.)*

BIANCA. This is from a film that was a big hit in China. Or was it Taiwan? I always get those two mixed up. Some place where they had a lot of spicy orange chicken. Anyway, in this country, it was released as "Attack of the Bug Creatures From Hell."

*(Dressed in tiny bikinis, the three **QUEENS** are poolside, splashing, blowing bubbles, laughing. A giant ant crawls out of the woods and drags **RICHELLE** out of*

frame. After a few beats, **ALEXIS** *and* **BIANCA** *are del-uged with blood and guts flying in from off camera.)*

ALEXIS. It took forever to wash that crap out of my hair. This one we sort of regret making, but it's always been very popular with you fans, thank you very much! "Cheerleader Summer Camp Blood Orgy."

(Dressed as cheerleaders, the three **QUEENS** *are prac-ticing a routine with a few other girls on an outdoor basketball court. A masked killer with a chainsaw spies on them from the bushes. The camera switches to the killer's POV as he runs towards them and we see severed body parts, pom-poms, skirts and sneakers and geysers of blood flying in and out of frame. A severed forearm and hand still clutching a pom-pom twitches on the ground.)*

ADDITIONAL AUTHOR'S NOTES:

If you use a very large front projection screen upstage (with a video projector mounted in the lighting grid out front) you may want to fill that blank space with additional still and animated projections at various other times during the show; e.g. a "Scream Queens" logo or ScreamiCon artwork, a video montage of her Hollywood headshots for "Fay Wray," stills or video clips of various "Jason," "Freddie" or "Michael Myers"-type killers during "Gotcha Cornered," kaleidoscopic effects for "Still in Demand," a cartoonish barnyard for "I'm Alright, Momma" or an animated landscape for the van ride in "South of the Border," etc.

For the various "gore" gags in "Special FX," consult with a local magician, make-up designer at a local college theatre department or costume store, or any avid horror movie fan. They should be able to help you execute different make-up effects and illusions that will startle the audience while still getting laughs because of the over-the-top outrageousness of seeing the stunts live.

Unless you're allowing a "splash zone" for your audience, be careful to contain the gore on the stage and away from the Queens. They need to perform two more songs after "Special FX" and you probably won't want to dry clean their costumes after every performance.

Feel free to decorate your theatre lobby and auditorium as if it were part of the ScreamiCon convention: movie posters, videos, horror and sci-fi merchandise that can be found at most comic book stores or on the internet. Perhaps a local merchant would like to set up a concession table and actually sell his horror memorabilia and collectibles. If your budget allows, make more of your own SCREAM QUEENS merchandise: posters, headshots, trading cards, calendars featuring your actresses.

Audio and video recordings of your production of SCREAM QUEENS – THE MUSICAL are strictly prohibited. However, you may want to make extended versions of the original videos you produce for the "demos" and sell your own.

Finally, the use of the prop CD boom box is entirely at the Director's option. It is not a requirement of the production, merely a suggestion. If you choose not to use the prop, ignore all stage directions about pushing buttons on and off. If you use live musicians, the prop is completely unnecessary.

SPECIAL PRE-RECORDED SOUND EFFECTS:

Auditorium door opening, sounds of a crowded bowling alley;

Auditorium door slams shut;

Cell phone rings several times;

Scratchy old recording of a "Pomp and Circumstance"-like theme; *(or see Piano Score)*

Scratchy old recording of a regal brass fanfare or vaudeville-like intro; *(or see Piano Score)*

Auditorium door opening, sounds of people singing and an accordion playing a polka;

"BORDER" VIDEO

This is an optional video bonus stunt if you have the budget and skills to pull it off.

While the audience ghouls are chasing the QUEENS during the musical underscoring sequence, a video cameraman joins the chase and shoots head-on close-ups of the snarling ghouls.

Then during the next 20 minutes of the show, a video editor backstage dubs these shots into some pre-existing footage of the QUEENS running from other zombie extras wearing the same sombreros and serapes in some exterior location.

This footage can then be the last clip etc. on the RICHELLE/ALEXIS/ BIANCA DEMO REEL as an excerpt from "Revenge of the Psycho Bimbos" where we see the scene shot earlier in the show with close-ups of the audience members as the zombies.

COSTUME PLOT

Primary for all characters:

As sexy and evocative as you can get away with; anything from Victoria's Secret to trashy punk lingerie; any variety of styles, colors, textures, from skimpy tops to short skirts to spike heels; as long as your actresses are comfortable wearing them and your audience is comfortable seeing them. Perhaps the Queens could be dressed as specific characters from some of their films; e.g. Tonya as a cheerleader, DeeDee as a dominatrix, Bianca as a surfer girl, Alexis in a business suit coat or white lab coat and stockings, Nadine in a slinky cocktail gown, Richelle as a Catholic schoolgirl. There is at least one opportunity during the show for each character to make a complete change offstage to a secondary costume. Mix and match. Remember that the Queens know that they are the sexual fantasies of the adolescent boys who are the "fans" attending the ScreamiCon and they play that attraction to the max.

Special costumes:

"Gotcha Cornered"	tight or spandex workout clothes: Bianca, DeeDee, Richelle
"Still In Demand"	anything to add to the campiness of the Busby Berkeley-like finale: Richelle, Bianca, DeeDee, Tonya, Alexis
"Everybody Starts At The Bottom"	The Supremes; dresses and wigs: Alexis, DeeDee, Bianca
"I'm Alright, Momma"	"Hee-Haw" type gingham dress: Bianca; old farmer and his wife: Tonya and Nadine other farm girls (Director's option): DeeDee, Alexis, Richelle
"South of the Border"	"Carmen Miranda" accessories, fruity hat: Alexis large sombreros and serapes: DeeDee, Nadine, Tonya, Richelle, Bianca
"Roger Corman"	wrap-around 50's poodle skirts: DeeDee, Nadine, Tonya, Alexis, Richelle
Bride of Frankenstein	wig, long white robe: Alexis;
Fifty Foot Woman	small top and mini-skirt made from white bed-sheet: Tonya;
Janet Leigh	flesh-colored leotard or body-suit: Richelle;
Video demos	whatever the scripts call for;

AND of course anything else that your Director, Choreographer and Designers think will add to the visual comedy of the show.

PROPS

The Set: *(on center table)*
Various 8x10 B&W headshots of the Queens
Small stand-up placecards with the Queens' names
Personal water bottles, tissues, Sharpie pens as needed
CD boom box *(optional)* on the center table or on a pedestal at the side
Small box of "Scream Queens' Throat Lozenges;" *(new box for each performance)*
4 plastic long-handled, double-headed axes (pre-set under table)

The Queens:
6 large tote bags or stylish carry-all purses, each containing personal items that they'll use during the show:
    6 cell phones, *(all)*
    make-up effects for "Special FX" *(all)*
    feminine items and Roger Corman trophy *(DeeDee)*
    Neiman-Marcus *(or high-end department store)* bag with three letters in envelopes and bloody fake ear, small whiskey flask *(Nadine)*
    sample DVD case *(Richelle)*
    small movie clapboard *(Alexis)*

Offstage:
5 or 6 small plush toy gorillas; the cuter, the better
large movie posters or photo blow-ups mounted on stiff cardboard of the "Bride of Frankenstein," "Attack of the Fifty Foot Woman," and Janet Leigh in the "Psycho" shower scene
various props and costume pieces for campy Busby-Berkeley finale of "Still in Demand"; e.g., feather boas, confetti, glitter, hand mirrors, bubbles, streamers, etc.
small toy car for Fifty Foot Woman
letter in envelope, ugly eye-glass frames for Bianca
small bible, corncob pipe for "Ma"
pitchfork, cancelled check for "Pa"
small piece of paper for DeeDee; *(message received backstage)*
5 Halloween masks; *(specific characters are Director's choice)*
clear plastic shower curtain for Richelle
small water spray bottle for Tonya
small piece of paper for Richelle; *(message received backstage)*
life-size cardboard stand-up of Roger Corman; color or B&W
8x11 piece of Fax paper for Nadine *(message received backstage)*
larger and additional make-up effects for "Special FX"

Video demos:
whatever the scripts call for

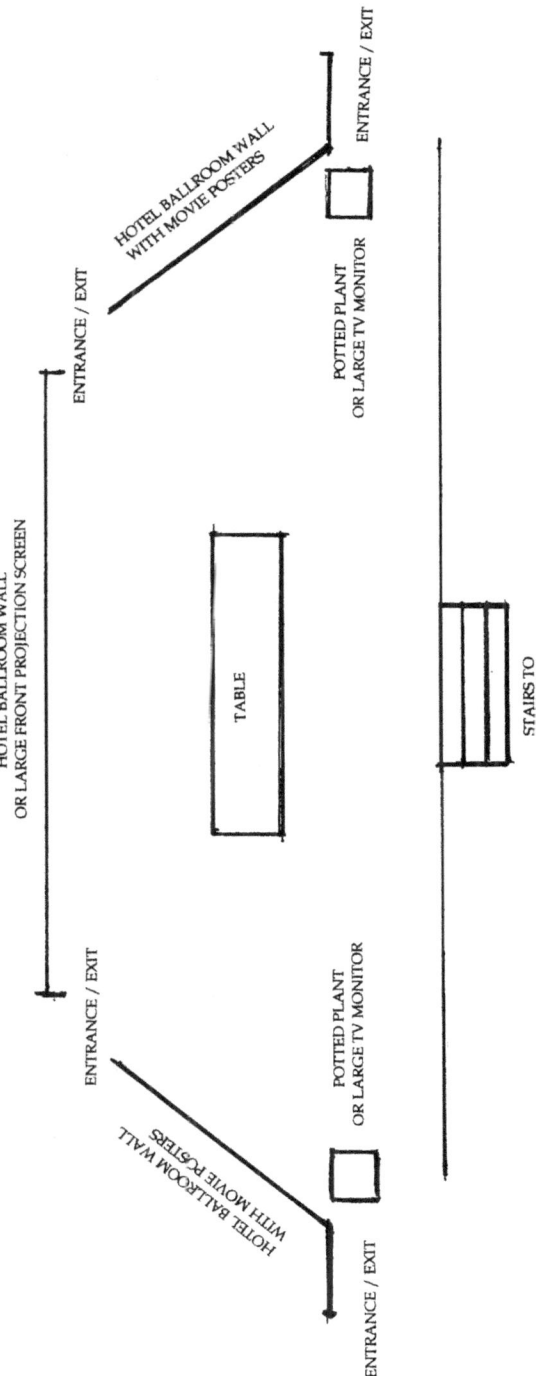

SET DESIGN FOR "SCREAM QUEENS – THE MUSICAL"

HOTEL BALLROOM WALL
WITH MOVIE POSTERS

ENTRANCE / EXIT

POTTED PLANT
OR LARGE TV MONITOR

ENTRANCE / EXIT

HOTEL BALLROOM WALL
OR LARGE FRONT PROJECTION SCREEN

TABLE

ENTRANCE / EXIT

STAIRS TO
AUDIENCE

POTTED PLANT
OR LARGE TV MONITOR

HOTEL BALLROOM WALL
WITH MOVIE POSTERS

ENTRANCE / EXIT

www.ingramcontent.com/pod-product-compliance
Lightning Source LLC
Chambersburg PA
CBHW070646120726
47909CB00004B/1608